It was the skeleton of Fastred all right, clad in armor, helm, and rotting boots. The gray day illuminated him poorly, but twin fires burned in the hollow eye sockets. The glare held me captive, and I could only watch as he began to ascend the stairs, the leather strips of boot dropping aside as the bony toes dug into the moss. I knew that I would stand there until he was at the top of the stairs, taking my thin neck between his finger bones and squeezing and squeezing until my eyes were as big as saucers, saucers popping right out of my head. . . .

Fantasy Mysteries from TSR

Murder in Cormyr
Chet Williamson
A FORGOTTEN REALMS® Mystery

Murder in Tarsis
John Maddox Roberts
A DRAGONLANCE® Mystery

Murder in Halruaa
Richard S. Meyer
A FORGOTTEN REALMS Mystery

MURDER
IN
CORMYR

Chet Williamson

Paul and Louise McCandless, with love

MURDER IN CORMYR
©1998 TSR, Inc.
All Rights Reserved.

Distributed to the book trade in the United States by Random House, Inc. and in Canada by Random House of Canada, Ltd.

Distributed to the hobby, toy, and comic trade in the United States and Canada by regional distributors.

Distributed worldwide by Wizards of the Coast, Inc. and regional distributors.

FORGOTTEN REALMS and the TSR logo are registered trademarks owned by TSR, Inc.

All TSR characters, character names, and the distinctive likenesses thereof are trademarks owned by TSR, Inc.

TSR, Inc., a subsidiary of Wizards of the Coast, Inc.
Made in the U.S.A.

Cover art by Larry Elmore
First Printing: March 1996
First Paperback Edition: July 1998
Library of Congress Catalog Card Number: 96-60827

9 8 7 6 5 4 3 2 1

ISBN: 0-7869-1173-5
8655PXXX1501

U.S., CANADA,
ASIA, PACIFIC, & LATIN AMERICA
Wizards of the Coast, Inc.
P.O. Box 707
Renton, WA 98057-0707
+1-206-624-0933

EUROPEAN HEADQUARTERS
Wizards of the Coast, Belgium
P.B. 34
2300 Turnhout
Belgium
+32-14-44-30-44

Visit our web site at **www.tsr.com**

1

I don't know what was more alarming that autumn in Ghars-the drought, the roving agents of the Zhentarim and the Iron Throne, the ghost, or the upcoming visit of the Grand Council of Cormyr's Merchants' Guild.

In retrospect, I guess it was the murders.

Not that those other occurrences weren't matters for concern. The farms around Ghars had had no rain for weeks. Most of the wells had dried up, the crops were scanty, and the local squires were eyeing their account books the way a hungry man looks at the broken woodwork of his false teeth, with much dismay and worry over what comes next.

What water remained was diverted into a public cistern, a huge wooden tank zealously guarded by Khlerat, the nearsighted retiree who served as Ghars's unofficial master of public works. And since Ghars is a market town that serves a farming community, a long dry spell was about as welcome a visitor as a slimy Zhentarim agent at a meeting of Cormyr's War Wizards.

Speaking of slimy Zhentarim agents, the crack contingent of Purple Dragons stationed in Ghars had apprehended two of them in as many months, no doubt plotting to invade Cormyr, overthrow King Azoun, or at the very least assassinate some noble of renown. They're like that.

The Dragons also captured one agent of the Iron Throne secret society, a group that I viewed as far less of a threat. I mean, come now—a secret society of *merchants*? Ooo, scary . . . Still, Azoun had banished them from the kingdom for a year, so he must have had a good reason.

By the second week of Eleint, I was wishing that he would have banished the Cormyrean Merchants' Guild along with their wicked Iron Throne counterparts. Every other word out of the mouths of the local merchants and farmers concerned how honored little Ghars was to host the high mucky-mucks of the guild a few days hence.

My master's taciturn ways seemed most welcome after a shopping trip to the town, where the greengrocer and the butcher and the clothier would natter on for hours about the guild council's eagerly anticipated arrival. What the big deal was I didn't know, since if these officials were like most merchants I'd known, they'd be sour of face, tight with their purse strings, and sober as judges.

And pale as ghosts, most of them, which brings us to the subject on the minds of most of the residents. *Fastred's* ghost, to be exact. To give you the proper *spirit* of things, pun most definitely intended, let me quote from a writer far more highly skilled than myself—that great historian Carcroft the Long, who, in his *Anthropologic and Folkloric Historie of the Settled Lands* (Volume III), states:

> And in those dayes in the lande between Sembia and Cormyr, there dwelt within the Vaste Swamppe a reaver and a chieftain hight FASTRED. He lived in the swamppe with his people, heedless of the monstyrs and beasties that also resided therein, such as the men lyke unto lizardes, the goblynnes and trolles and grelles.
>
> He and his band of cuthroattes and murtherers would sweepe down upon the caravans that travelled the Way of the Manticore, lootyng them of gemmes, gold, and silvyr. With his greate battle axe would he cleave in twaine those who refused to yielde to him and his reavers.
>
> Though he was pursued, e'en by smalle armies, his knowledge of the Vaste Swamppe was so greate that he lost his pursuers alwaie, kenning solidde lande where others saw only mucke, into which the hooves of their steedes would sinke and they would quickly drowne.
>
> Fastred lived as a kinge within the Vaste Swamppe for many yeares, protected by the treacherous sands and mucke that surrounded him, until Deathe came upon him, from whose fell clutche was no escape. Halfe his treasures did he bequeath to his warriors to share amongst them, while the other halfe, wealthe beyond measure, was sealed with him in his tombe, an isle of rocke in the swamppe.
>
> It is told by those in the districte how his glowwing ghoste, stille yclad in armor and bearing his greate axe, guards his hoarde, threatening any who may come nigh by mischance or by purpose. Of all the terrors of the Vaste Swamppe, those who dwell in the Settled Landes do agree that Fastred's Ghoste is the moste to be feared.

And that's that. A bit old-fashioned, and I wouldn't

give a copper for his spelling, but Carcroft sums it up pretty neatly. A hidden treasure in the swamp and a glowing, protective ghost with an axe. There—I think I just summed it up even more neatly, and my spelling's better too.

Though *why* this ghost was "moste to be feared," I couldn't have told you. As far as I knew, he had never actually severed anyone in two with that big axe of his, and the Vast Swamp has more real horrors than you can shake a stick at. Along with the lizard men, goblins, trolls, and grells that old Carcroft mentioned, there are also dragons, meazels, hydrae, beholders, and probably even the occasional tax-gatherer, so a simple axe-wielding ghost doesn't seem too daunting.

But you wouldn't have thought it from the reaction he got in Ghars once a few people started spotting him on the edge of the Vast Swamp after nightfall, his gaunt face glowing green, his ancient armor shining on his massive body, swinging his axe and coming toward them like the inexorable death that awaits us all, the death that had claimed him centuries ago.

And the death that claimed him again, this time wearing the grim face of murder.

2

But I'm getting ahead of myself, which is something that I'm apt to do. If my master Benelaius has told me once, he's told me a thousand times, "Jasper, put your mind and your thoughts in order, or the results will be ordure." And since he has given me permission to record his activities in this particular matter for posterity, I shouldn't jump about like a rabid feystag but should take matters as they came.

So, from the beginning.

My grandfather was born in a little log hut. . . .

Well, perhaps not quite so far back a beginning, although knowing about my grandfather leads to why I became Benelaius's indentured servant. Old Grandpaw Hurthkin was a halfling, you see, one of those little people whose primary joy in life is taking advantage of humans. He took advantage of the human Guirath Moondock by running away with and marrying his daughter, a woman so small she seemed near halfling herself.

Chet Williamson

The result of that union was my mother, a petite woman herself but with qualities more human than halfling. My father was human, so I am only one quarter halfling. And before you think of me as an eighthling, let me tell you that I have heard that old wheeze told by innumerable drunken wits in an infinitude of taverns. Spare me this time.

My possession of halfling blood was what led me to try to burgle the wizard Benelaius's house, and that sorry attempt was what got me . . .

Ah, but there I go again. An arrow-straight, nondivergent narrative, that's the ticket.

I and some of the other local lads were wondering about the old man who had just come to live on the outskirts of Ghars. He was more than an old man, really. I had heard that he was one of Cormyr's War Wizards who had for some reason chosen to retire to this unspeakably weary little town and environs. I couldn't have vouched for it myself. My knowledge of Cormyrean public servants was limited to King Azoun, Sarp Redbeard, and Ghars's own Mayor Tobald, who, as far as I could see, did nothing but chuckle at babies and pretty girls and cut ribbons to open the occasional new store.

I had only a rough idea of what the College of War Wizards did. I pictured them as patriarchal old duffs who, when Cormyr went to war with one of its neighbors, would rain down magical thunder and lightning on the heads of the enemy. And I pictured this retired codger as someone *older* than old, a creaky relic who had lost his magic and just sat around hoping to shift his bowels once a week.

So when my chums expressed their fear of this new neighbor, I was quick to scoff. "Afraid of an old geezer?" I said. "What a bunch of lily-flowers!"

"Lily-flowers are we?" said Cedric Buckenwing.

"And I guess you'd be anxious to go and make this wizard's acquaintance, would you? You're that brave, are you, Jasper?"

I wasn't that brave, but I was that foolish. I had no one to say me nay, since I was of age, my mother had died that spring (my old man had been crushed by a wagon when I was seven), and I was working as a slop boy at the Sheaf of Wheat and sleeping in the buttery. I guess I was about as bright as the usual slop boy too, since I didn't finesse my way out of the situation but dug myself in deeper.

"To walk up to his door and bid him good day?" I said. "Why would I want to do that? There's no profit in it. But to enter his house by stealth"—I nodded sagely—"there's a *real* thrill."

I was proud of my halfling blood, you see, and, although I had done no more mischief than most young men my age, I allowed my friends to think that I was the scourge of Cormyr, burgling manor and merchant alike with my halfling skills. Why they should have believed this, since I was as impoverished as any other slop boy, I'll never know. Perhaps they only humored me. But this time Cedric was going to put me to the test.

"All right then," he slurred, the smell of cheap beer on his breath. "Let's go out to this old bloke's house, and you can prove what a great burglar you are once and for all."

And take me for a turnip if I didn't agree to do it. I had fantasized about the romance of thievery for so long that it seemed to me a chance to realize my destiny.

We waited until night, then rode out, two to a mount, to the edge of the Vast Swamp where this wizard had had his cottage built. To me, the location was another sign of addlepatedness, since the dangers of the Vast Swamp were all too real. I was more concerned about what might be lurking in the darkness around the cottage than in the dwelling itself.

But we made the ride unscathed, and left the horses a good quarter mile from the cottage. I was to go the rest of the way on foot, break in, take something to prove it, and return to my friends, who, if they had been real friends, wouldn't have let me do such an idiotic thing in the first place.

3

A sickly, gibbous moon pushed its weak rays through the thick mist that lay over the ground like a mildewed blanket. I could barely see my feet in front of me as I crept toward the spot where I thought the cottage would be.

Despite the drought, the ground near the swamp squelched underfoot, so that my worn shoes made a soft sucking noise with each step, a sound impossible to prevent. Although the time of summer's fading had come, the heat near the swamp was oppressive, and I imagined the Vast Swamp as a huge graveyard filled with dead things, the heat caused by their slow, miasmic rotting.

With such pleasant thoughts in my head, I was almost glad to see the outlines of the dwelling I was supposed to break into. In truth, it looked more like a large farmhouse than a cottage, but I thought that might have been a trick of the night and my imagination. No light shone through the windows of the two-story structure, and I went around to the rear of the house, which unfortunately looked out upon the swamp.

I paused for several minutes, looking into the darkness in the direction of the Vast Swamp. Seeing nothing and hearing only the sounds of night insects, I turned my attention back to the cottage. A back door that I assumed led to the kitchen was locked. But a window had been left slightly open. The opening was not large enough for a full-grown man to get through, but it proved no obstacle to a spindly young man with halfling blood.

In a trice I was in a small room in which I could vaguely make out several baskets of apples and shelves with jars of food. Again I listened for sounds of alarm, but heard nothing. I thought of taking a jar and scuttling back out the window but was sure that Cedric would mock me, suggesting that I had merely rifled an outbuilding. Besides, my presence in a place where I most definitely should not be emboldened me, and my heart pounded in an ecstasy of fearful and excited joy. I had to explore farther. I was a rogue, a thief, a night stalker . . .

An idiot.

A small kitchen, as I had guessed, lay beyond the open doorway, and I felt my way around its perimeter until my fingertips brushed against the wood of a door. I pushed gently and followed it as it swung into another room.

I didn't have to worry about light here. The coals from a dying fire on the hearth lit the large room with a dim red glow, and although the absence of insect songs indicated no windows were open, the temperature was comfortable, as if the muggy warmth were commanded to remain outside.

In the weak light, I could make out several pieces

of what looked like large, overstuffed furniture. On them, and on the floor near the fire, were dozens of what looked like round or oval cushions. On many of these I saw what I took to be metal or glass buttons reflecting the red coals' light. Here, I thought, was an old man who liked his comforts—wall to wall cushions so that he could plop his tired body down whenever the desire took him.

One of these cushions, I realized, would be the perfect thing to take. There were so many that one would probably never be missed, and therefore there would be no pursuit. Yet a cushion was a personal and homely enough thing to offer as proof to my friends that I had indeed breached the wizard's sanctum. I selected a particularly fluffy-looking one on the outskirts of the fire's glow, where its absence would not be noted, and reached down and grabbed it, sinking my fingers into its puffy depths.

The scream that ensued was even louder than my own. The pillow twisted and writhed in my hand, and grew teeth and claws that savaged the soft flesh of my palm and fingers and wrist.

I shook my hand desperately, and the creature dropped to the carpet, where it made one final, blood-drawing slash at my ankle and retreated, its eyes still on me, its back arched, and the fur along its spine standing straight up. Its hiss was swallowed up by the deep, throaty growls that filled the room as thickly as what I had mistaken for cushions.

Every one was a cat, a cat that had been curled and resting, but with one or two glasslike eyes open, watching the interloper foolish enough to enter their master's home. Dozens upon dozens of cushiony cats, that now uncurled their bodies as one, their eyes and fangs glaring, hundreds of razor-sharp claws unsheathed to slice to ribbons the stranger in their midst.

Chet Williamson

I could not move, and, aside from my first shriek of horror when the cat had come to life in my hands, could not utter a sound. If the door at the far wall hadn't opened, I think those cats and I might still be there, growing old together.

But the door did open, and a blinding glare of light fell through it onto the cats and me. In the center of that light, his round body casting a great shadow on the floor and at least a dozen spitting cats, was the wizard, in the company of still more cats, one perched upon his shoulder, and one in his arms, too happy with the stroking it was receiving to take notice of me.

The wizard took notice, however. In a voice as rich and plummy as a pudding, he chuckled, then said, "Well, I see we have a visitor, my friends . . . a welcoming committee, mayhap?"

His furry feline friends eased up on the spitting and hissing. I thought I even heard a few purrs due to his presence, though I noticed in the brighter light that the cats' claws remained dangerously unsheathed. The wizard went on.

"As you see, O stranger, I bear no weapon. Yet"—he gestured with his petting hand to the cats—"I have nearly a hundred at my beck and call. If you give me your word you shall neither fight nor flee, I shall ease their suspicious minds."

It took me several tries to get out the words. "I . . . I swear."

"That is quite decent of you," said the wizard, and then he looked at the cats, just looked at them in a not particularly stern or demanding way, but it was as though I were suddenly one of the family. The growling ceased on the instant, and I was nearly knocked off my feet by a multitude of fuzzy backs and legs rubbing up against my ankles, one of which still oozed blood.

"They seem to be good judges of character," the wizard said, still patting the cat in his arms, "despite their guardian proclivities. Once they are assured there is no danger to me, they treat the interloper fairly. Were you truly an evil man, bent upon my destruction, they would still be on their guard, watching you every second. So, even though you have broken in here illegally, you strike them as an honest fellow. Quite a paradox. Honest but ill-advised, perhaps?"

I shrugged. I didn't know what to say. Here I was, caught red-handed (literally, I thought, wiping blood from my fingers) burglarizing the abode of a retired War Wizard. I was nearly aghast at my own stupidity—and ill luck.

"Put a few logs on the fire, stranger," the wizard said, sitting down in a chair large enough to hold his heavy frame. Immediately a score of cats sought the comfort of his capacious lap, and he chuckled again, accommodating as many as he could and gently shooing the rest to the floor.

"You'll find a teapot on the hearth. There's tea in the kitchen. Fetch it, put some water on the fire, and we'll have a cup together."

He didn't caution me not to run away, but he didn't have to. A dozen of his cats came along with me, and I had the feeling that if I had made any move to escape, we would have been joined by the others. By candlelight, I found the tea, returned to the wizard, and before too long was sitting across from him, sipping a very good cup of tea, if I say so myself.

Benelaius took a sip and nodded appreciatively. "So tell me, what prompted you to enter my house?"

There was no point in a lie, since I felt he would have quickly detected one. "A dare," I said shame-facedly. "I was just supposed to come in, take something, and leave. But I picked up a cat by mistake."

"Had I not entered when I did," the wizard said, "they might have harmed you. Irreparably. Burglary is a crime, you know."

"I know, sir."

"I should by all rights turn you over to the authorities. You would undoubtedly serve a prison term. And then you would be released, hardened, made even stupider than you are, and probably become a professional thief, in and out of prison until one of your victims finally puts you out of your misery. *Or . . .*"

He cocked his head. "You could reform yourself, with my aid of course. You brew a decent cup of tea. What work do you do?"

"I'm slop boy at an inn in Ghars."

"Slop boy," he repeated thoughtfully, stroking a cat with one hand and his long gray beard with the other, while the cup and saucer trembled on his broad belly. "Then domestic service to a gentleman such as myself would be a step up. I need someone to run my errands to town and keep the cottage clean and running . . . and to look after the cats. I've hesitated because of the expense, but . . ."

He eyed me for a moment, and the intensity of his gaze belied his easy manner of speech. I felt as though he were peering into my brain, plucking out the thoughts and examining them. At last he spoke again.

"What's your name?"

"Jasper," I said.

"All right, Jasper, my name is Benelaius, and here is my proposition. I give you two options. Option one, I turn you over to the Purple Dragon contingent and tell them I caught you burglarizing my house, which, as we both know, is the truth. Option two, you agree to become my indentured servant for a period of, say, one year. You do whatever I tell you to do—go, fetch, clean, carry, cook—for which you will receive your room and board, and an education."

"An . . . education? You mean I'd have to take lessons?"

"Yes. Tutoring. From me, in lieu of a salary."

"So my options," I said, "are either jail or slavery."

He frowned. "The kingdom of Cormyr does not sanction slavery, as well you know."

"Well, what do you call working for you for a year for free?" I was bolder than I should have been, but since there was no option concerning being shredded by cats, I felt a bit braver.

Benelaius frowned even more deeply. "Perhaps a very *small* salary, then, to assist you in learning the management of your own money. How much do you earn at the inn?"

"Five silver falcons a month," I lied. I made only two a month.

"You lie," Benelaius said smoothly. "You make two at most, and I will pay you one. My tutelage will be worth many times that, and if you don't find a way to make your knowledge pay, it will be your own fault—assuming, that is, that you will want to leave at the end of the agreed upon term of service."

"Oh, I will all right, *if* I decide to do it in the first place." I was feeling pretty cocky since cat teeth were out of the picture.

"If not, I hear Cormyrean prison food is delightful. All the fresh weevils and moldy bread you can eat— if the big boys don't take it from you first. And frankly, crushing rocks with hammers eighteen hours a day would put some muscle on that spindly frame. . . ."

Chet Williamson

I sighed and looked around at the cats who would be my roommates for the next year. "When do I start?" I asked.

4

I started the very next day. After signing the papers that Benelaius drew up, I went back to the Sheaf of Wheat to give my notice to Lukas Spoondrift and gather my belongings. Spoondrift, the owner of the Sheaf of Wheat, went into a mild rage when I told him I was leaving, and shouted at me unceasingly as I packed my few things.

But I made my escape without bloodshed—save for Spoondrift's sore throat—and eventually found myself ensconced in the wizard's household. And a fairly decent dwelling it was, if you disregard its proximity to a swamp where all sorts of monsters and, yes, ghosts trod the squishy terrain.

A small front hall led into the main room, where Benelaius's cats had captured me. It was pleasant by daylight, with two wide, high windows in the front, and another at the side. In the back was the kitchen, and off the main room was a spacious study with doors that opened onto a back porch that Benelaius called a piazza. Rustic wooden chairs were positioned so that the sitters could look out into the swamp, if such was their desire.

It certainly wasn't mine. The Vast Swamp gave me the creeps, even though Benelaius told me that he had cast a protective spell around his property. When I asked how I was able to get inside so easily, he told me that it wasn't worth the energy to cast a spell that kept out spindly servants. In fact, not doing so had *caught* him one, hadn't it?

I had to agree. But working for Benelaius wasn't all that bad. I slept in one of the three bedrooms upstairs. The large one was Benelaius's, of course; the next largest was for any guests he might have (and he had a surprising number); and the third was mine. It was the smallest, but much nicer than my pallet in the Sheaf of Wheat's buttery. A fourth room above stairs was used as a small library, stuffed so full of books that I feared the floor would collapse. The ceiling below did have a definite dip.

My duties were far from wearing. I cooked, cleaned, ran errands, bought groceries and whatever else was required around the house, emptied chamber pots, and took care of the cats. This last activity required less time than you would think.

The thought of cleaning up after nearly a hundred felines had initially made me shudder. But the cats were extremely deferential to my well-being, strolling off into the swamp when the call of nature arose. So the stench associated with multicat households was never the bane of ours. On the contrary, the cats were polite, even affectionate to me now that I was no longer a stranger, and I enjoyed their company, once the feeding and milk-drawing was finished.

True to his word, Benelaius tutored me for at least

an hour each day, in the midmorning after I had finished washing the breakfast dishes and airing the beds. He was pleased to find that I already knew how to read (my mother had taught me), and he covered many subjects, of which wizardry was never one. I asked him why, one evening as we sat together by the fire, drowning comfortably in our sea of cats.

"Best not to know those things," he said. "Though the study of wizardry was my making, it also proved to be my downfall."

"What?" I asked. "I thought you retired from the College of War Wizards. Were you really kicked out?"

He summoned up enough energy to scowl at me. "No, my leaving was my own choice. I had had enough of magic. The downfall I mention was due merely to my own . . . dissatisfaction with magic."

"Dissatisfied? Why, I'd think it would be *great* to be a wizard. All you have to do is just wave your hand, say a few magic words, and presto, you get whatever you want!"

If you did not mark my naivete in the preceding speech, be certain that Benelaius did. "That's what you think, is it?" He gave a *tsk-tsk* and shook his craggy head. "Even the smallest spell, Jasper, takes great knowledge, greater preparation, and even greater energy. The power of magic saps you, drains you, and enchants you until you go to great magical lengths to do even the simplest things, tasks that would take you an iota of the strength to physically do yourself. I've seen it happen to others, and I found it happening to me.

"I decided that I would engage my mind in other interests—stop and smell the roses, if you will. And when I did, I found the natural world and its laws a delightful contrast to that of the supernatural. Over a period of months, I determined that I would give up magic unless its use was absolutely necessary, and live as others did—the natural life, studying and writing of such things until my knowledge of them became as great as it is of wizardry.

"I told my fellow War Wizards of my decision to leave their noble company. Some thought I was a fool. But others, like Vangerdahast, Chairman Emeritus of the College of War Wizards, and Royal Mage to King Azoun himself, thought me wise to follow my will. So I searched for a quiet place far from Suzail, where the War Wizards congregate, and here I am."

I still didn't get it. "But doesn't it get boring? I mean, I always thought that Ghars was the dullest spot in Cormyr, and after being a War Wizard and fighting battles and all, how can you stand living here?"

He rubbed Grimalkin's ears until the cat purred. I was starting to be able to tell the cats apart now. "Not all War Wizards see battle. I mostly conducted research into how to make spells more efficacious, and often worked healing spells when wounded warriors were brought back from the front line. Personally, I detest violence. . . ."

He did too. He seldom ate meat, and would do so only in order not to insult a guest who had brought along food and drink. We had a good many of those, mostly wizards come to see their old friend. Once even Vangerdahast paid a surprise visit. I laid as low as possible, fearful that the stern and powerful old man would turn me into a slug if I were to pour a drop of tea into his saucer instead of his cup.

Afterward Benelaius confided to me that Vangerdahast often paid surprise visits to retired wizards, War Wizards in particular, just to let them know that he still had his eye on them should they intend to use their wizardry for evil ends. But when the

Royal Mage took his leave of Benelaius, I heard him say to my master, "I know I need not keep track of your doings, old friend, but were I not to plague you as well with a visit, all other wizards might think you my pet. Besides, I've missed your company."

So I could only assume that Vangerdahast had a soft spot for my master, for which I was glad. It's not nice to have the most powerful mage in the realm eyeing you askance—or eying you in any way, for that matter.

But even with wizardly visits and my daily chores, I still had much time to myself. Since I had to be close at hand, I passed that time the only way I could, by reading the multitudinous volumes that filled the second-floor library, since the books in Benelaius's study were off limits. Don't think that they were forbidden volumes of necromancy and chiromancy and whatever other mancys there might be. Most of them were terribly complex books dealing with the natural sciences, and I was forbidden them because if I were to get any out of the seemingly random order in which my master had them, his research, so he claimed, might be put back days or even weeks.

Sure, I thought, but I left them alone, and dusted carefully around their perimeters. I had plenty of other things to read.

And read I did, both nonfiction and fiction. Benelaius had no cheap romances on his shelves, however. Instead I immersed my mind in the literary masterpieces of Faerûn—Kastor's *Archetymbal*, the *Proceedings* of Magus Firewand, Kirkabey's *Mediations and Meditations*, and Chelm Vandor's *Seasons in the Heartlands*. Besides these acclaimed classics, there were others, books of philosophy, epic poems, tales of travel, and I devoured them all, liking some more than others.

But the volume that I most delighted in was the one that my master most scorned. It had been left behind by a visiting mage "in his dotage," Benelaius insisted. "Why else would he have read such drivel?"

I found the drivel fascinating. It was a thin book bound in cheap felt called The *Adventures of Camber Fosrick*, written by Lodevin Parkar. In it were half a dozen thrilling tales of the great "consulting cogitator," Camber Fosrick, who could solve any mystery, bringing the darkest corners of crime to blazing light through his brilliant deductive reasoning. The stories of robbery, smuggling, and even murder held me spellbound, and I read them over and over again, enchanted as much by the character of Camber Fosrick as by the intricate plots he successfully worked out.

"You'll rot your brain with that tripe," Benelaius said whenever he saw me with the book.

"On the contrary," I argued, "this is quite good stuff, master. Deductive reasoning, logic, using disparate clues to come to a reasoned conclusion—the same sort of thing found in Trelaphin's *Thought and Its Processes*."

"Theft, rapine, and slaughter!" thundered Benelaius as best as a man practically wider than he is tall could thunder. Needless to say, this was one literary subject on which we did not see eye to eye.

But I did as he said, and continued to read and learn, and after I had been with him the better part of a year, I began to yearn even more for my freedom. With the knowledge I had accrued from his lessons and books, I was sure I could make a grand start for myself in the world, perhaps as a scribe, for my writing and my method of expressing myself had increased a hundredfold under his tutelage. So I couldn't wait for the year to be up and my indentureship to come to an end.

Benelaius occasionally hinted at what my future plans might be, suggesting that perhaps I might like to stay with him, at a slight increase in salary. But my pursed lips and slight smile told him unmistakably that I wanted to be his servant no longer, no matter how much he had come to depend on me. There were other potential slop boys about, and I was sure he would be able to lure one into his service. I was bound for the great world of Faerûn, to see all the things I had only read about, and to seek my destiny.

5

My heart was growing lighter this Eleint, despite the drought, the ghost, and the secret agents populating the land. For in only four more days I would be free. Still, my time was not yet up, and I had decided to serve Benelaius faithfully to the end. For one reason, he had always treated me fairly, and for another, I did not want any slippage on my part to warrant his demand of a legal extension of my services due to some loophole in our agreement. I simply did as I was told, served him well, and waited for my deliverance.

So when Benelaius gave me two golden lions and told me to go into Ghars to get a cask of clarry, I sprang to my task, despite my discomfort at having to return in darkness. "I'm sorry to make you go out now," he said, "but I just realized that I had no spirits at all for Lindavar's visit on the morrow, and he was terribly fond of clarry back in Suzail." He slipped me an extra half falcon. "Have something for yourself as

24

well, but don't drink enough to prevent your return sometime before dawn, yes?"

I knew he was joking. I cared little for spirits, though perhaps if I had had more familiarity with them, things might have been different. You don't become a drunkard on one silver falcon a month. A pauper perhaps, but not a drunkard.

My master had two horses in his small stable. Jenkus could be saddled and ridden and set a good pace, but the huge and ill-tempered Stubbins would throw any rider. He was good only in harness. Benelaius used the two horses to pull his carriage on the rare occasions when he left the cottage. I thought he would likely have crushed any single mount.

As Jenkus trotted toward Ghars, I wondered what else Benelaius might have forgotten that Lindavar required. The young mage had never visited Benelaius, though they corresponded frequently. A week seldom went by without an exchange of letters between the two, and from the thickness of the envelopes that I carried back and forth to the messenger service in Ghars, they were quite long.

Lindavar was Benelaius's handpicked successor in the College of War Wizards. My master confided to me that his former pupil was having some "problems of a professional nature," and that was the reason for the visit. I confess that I felt only indifference for Lindavar's plight, and looked on his visit as primarily an inconvenience, although my extra busyness would help keep my impatience for freedom at bay.

But as I rode west toward Ghars, the Vast Swamp on my left growing more and more distant, I thought about neither Lindavar nor my freedom, but of Fastred's ghost, and prayed that I would not be confronted by the sight of it as I returned home that evening. A great many people around Ghars had seen it, and it seemed to haunt the northwest swamp-side. It was, if the stories were true, easily seen from the road that connected the farms on the swamp's north and west with each other and Ghars.

Farmers returning home late from market had spotted it, as had weary drinkers leaving the Swamp Rat, a tavern recently opened to quench the thirsts of those farmers who didn't like having to ride all the way into Ghars for an ale and companionship. Unfortunately, the Swamp Rat's business had fallen off severely after the appearance of Fastred's specter. Even Mayor Tobald himself, coming back from a dinner with the Rambeltook family, had come across the threatening revenant.

Even though no one had claimed to see the creature in the daylight, I still breathed a sigh of relief when I struck the fork in the road. I turned north-west toward town, and saw no one on the southwest road that led to the farms on the west of the swamp.

Another twenty minutes brought me to Ghars. The first thing an approaching rider noticed was the large cistern that had been built once the drought had gained its dry and dusty foothold. This was nothing more than a gigantic barrel on stilts, really, but it was the tallest edifice in town, and water from every producing well in the area was brought to it.

I rode past Aunsible Durn's smithy and stables, and saw him still at work, banging away at something on his anvil. Whether he was making horseshoes or plowshares, or one of the more impractical products of his calling, I couldn't tell. Once Durn brought his impressive skills to Ghars, many of the local squires took a fancy to outfitting their farmhands with Durn's sturdy pikes and halberds, and themselves with fancy armor, just in case we should ever be invaded, you see. I've always believed that the squires, vain fools that they are, just liked to wear the armor on wedding and feast days.

I didn't see Dovo, Durn's large but less than breathtakingly brilliant assistant. Well, it was nearly six. Maybe Durn had let him off early. Or maybe he had just got tired of Dovo's idiotic presence.

The Bold Bard was the only place to purchase clarry. The Swamp Rat was much closer, but its inventory was limited to ale, beer, cider, and table wine fit only for cleaning paint brushes. The Bold Bard was surrounded by other buildings in the heart of Ghars, and I saw that it was already bustling, with merchants and farmers going in and coming out its door. The coming out was a bit more unsteady than the going in, a tribute to the power of the tavern's spirits.

I tied Jenkus to a stout post of the colonnade and went in to the common room. There I bought the cask of clarry and had Shortshanks, the dwarven owner and proprietor, place it behind the bar until I was ready to go. The air of camaraderie was contagious, and I sat at the bar and ordered a cod pie and a Golden Sands Orange, the sweetest, least bitter brew I knew of.

Thus fortified, I relaxed and watched the rest of the world go by, at least that part of it that lived in or stumbled into our little piece of it. The talk that wasn't about the Merchants' Guild council meeting seemed to be about the ghost.

"Ah, it's just an illusion," said the tailor. "People seeing things."

"You mean a *de*lusion, and it's not," said the chandler. "It's real, right enough. My Uncle Fendrake saw it oncet, years ago, and Uncle Fendrake never seen anything in his life that wasn't there."

"Dunno about that," returned the tailor. "He musta seen some beauty in your Aunt Magda. . . ."

Most, like the chandler, held out for the ghost's authenticity. It's not like there's never been a supernatural manifestation in Faerûn before, and there was no good reason *not* to believe in its existence.

The hubbub died down for a moment when Barthelm Meadowbrock came in. Though he was probably the richest merchant in town, the hush wasn't so much for him as for his daughter, Mayella. She was one of the fairest flowers of Cormyr, and when you added in her daddy's money, she became an even greater prize.

Hair as golden as corn silk, eyes as blue as the Dragonmere in summer, lips as red as . . . well, you get the general picture. Not a man in the Bold Bard did not wish himself in the place of the little lap dog that Mayella tenderly caressed. And along with her looks, she had a marvelous personality as well, though she always seemed a bit shadowed by the presence of her father.

That was no cause for wonder, since nearly *everyone* seemed shadowed by the presence of her father. He was a mountainous man, peaked with a wavy mop of hair that once must have been red-orange, but that was now diluted by white-blond hairs to the shade of the Sheaf of Wheat's butter-tomato soup. None of that particular dish's sweetness sat on him outwardly, however, for he was a most demanding man. Money can do that to a person. Or so I'm told.

Barthelm required the best table, the best bottle of mead, the most delectable viands, and the most scrupulous service possible, or the proprietor and everyone else within earshot would hear about it. He owned the local grist mill (ox driven, due to the shortage of running water, so he would never be impoverished by drought), as well as a fleet of fast wagons to take the produce he bought from the local farmers to Suzail and Marsember before it spoiled. In those cities, his agents sold the edibles for up to ten times what he had paid for them, and the buyers were glad to get them at any price.

But today I could see that Barthelm had more on his mind than finding a suitable suitor for his lovely daughter, or worrying about how the drought was going to affect his bottom line. In three days the Grand Council of Cormyr's Merchants' Guild, of which Barthelm was the district representative, would be coming to little Ghars for their annual meeting.

This important group, comprising the wealthiest and most powerful merchants in the realm, always met in one of Cormyr's major cities—Suzail or Arabel or Marsember. Occasionally they would deign to gather in a smaller resort town like Gladehap, for the fine food, drink and accommodations. But for them to gather in such a little rattrap as Ghars, where the forgettable fare at the Sheaf of Wheat and the Silver Scythe are the best to be offered . . . well, it was unheard of, and was a great testament to Barthelm Meadowbrock's perseverance.

But once the die was cast, Barthelm was going to leave nothing to chance. This meeting was going to be the best ever. The council would be lodged in both the Sheaf and the Scythe, since neither inn had enough rooms to accommodate them all, and Barthelm had, out of his own pocket, given Garnet Pennorth, owner of the Silver Scythe, enough gold to add a large and impressive meeting room onto his inn.

The merchant had likewise overseen every detail of the provisioning of the meeting's larder and cellar, including bringing in chefs from Suzail, and now his grumbling thunderclap of a voice called out to Shortshanks behind the bar. "Dwarf! Did you get the butt of Westgate Ruby that I ordered?"

"Coming in tomorrow," Shortshanks grumbled back. He didn't like being called "dwarf." In fact, he didn't like being called anything.

"It better," Barthelm said. "The welcoming dinner is Beef and Oysters Barnabas, and Westgate's the only wine to go with it."

Closer to the dwarf than Barthelm, I overheard Shortshanks's muttered comment as to what liquid Barthelm could drink with his Beef and Oysters Barnabas. I wasn't the only one, from the titters that swept down the bar. But Shortshanks didn't crack a smile. Dwarves, sullen and cranky as they are, are miserable choices for tavern keepers, but Shortshanks had come into possession of the Bold Bard by inheritance. It had been left to him by its former owner, a jolly gnome whose will said he bequeathed it to Shortshanks solely in the hopes that it would finally make the dwarf smile. It didn't work.

"Better watch your tongue, dwarf," said Barthelm, not as angry as he would have been had he actually heard the comment, "or I'll take my business to the Swamp Rat."

As he whirled round on the merchant, Shortshanks's expression changed from one who has bitten into a pickle to one who has just sucked up the entire barrel of brine. "The Swamp Rat?" the dwarf said with as much disgust as he could muster. "Aye, go there! Serve your fancy guests with sour cider, watered wine, and ale as flat as a duergar's head! I've known horses to make a better brew than Hesketh Pratt serves. And give my curse to Fastred's ghost on your way!"

With that final riposte, Shortshanks turned back to polishing his bar glasses, no doubt wishing they were gems from dwarven mines.

Barthelm, for once, contained his anger. He knew, as we all did, that he had touched a sore spot. Before Hesketh Pratt opened the Swamp Rat, Shortshanks's tavern was the only game in town for those who wanted an informal atmosphere in which to drink, since the Silver Scythe and the Sheaf of Wheat concentrate more on Ghars's definition of "fine dining," which basically means food that won't bite back. But the Swamp Rat had taken away much of Shortshanks's business, or at least it had until the ghost came along.

"Pretty full place tonight, Shortshanks," called out Tobald, the mayor of Ghars, as he strode into the tavern with a big, burly man I recognized but could not name.

Shortshanks, true to dwarven form, did not acknowledge Tobald's merry hail, but Tobald went on anyway, seating his slightly overweight frame in his usual booth and inhaling deeply the scent of tobacco smoke and rich ale with his red, bulbous nose. "That ghost must be good for business, eh? Scared the willies out of me, I'll tell you. I'll not ride that swamp road at night if I can help it."

Shortshanks gave a grunt, and that was good enough for Tobald, who began to speak cheerily to his companion.

"Who's that with Tobald?" I asked the tailor.

"You don't know Grodoveth?" he said, and the name rang a bell. "He's Azoun's envoy to this region. Brings the king and Sarp Redbeard news of everything between Thunderstone and Wheloon." Sarp Redbeard of Wheloon was our local lord, if over sixty miles away as the crow flies can still be "local."

31

Chet Williamson

The tailor leaned in closer to me and spoke so softly that I had to struggle to hear in the noisy tavern. "Related to the king, and yet he rides about from one small town to the next like any other low-grade civil servant. Funny one, you ask me. Pretty short, too."

"He looks quite tall to me," I said, eyeing Grodoveth.

"Not in stature," the tailor said wearily, "in *temper*. The royal crest had come off his cloak, and he had me sew it back on. This on a Sunday morn and me with a head that feels like an orc's been waltzing on it all night. So I sewed it a little crooked . . . just a *little* . . . and you'd have thought I had questioned his mother's honor. He threw the cloak back in my face and started to draw his blade, but I was able to . . . calm him down."

"By begging abjectly," added the chandler.

"Well, he may be short-tempered," I observed, "but he has good taste in the fairer sex."

While we were speaking, Grodoveth had gotten up and gone over, Tobald in his wake, to the table at which Mayella and her father were sitting. Tobald was the first to speak, however. "Barthelm! So good to see you this fine evening! And your lovely daughter too! Oh my, what a precious little doggie. I do so love animals, and they love me as well. Hello, my little precious . . ."

Tobald's charm must have failed him. As he put out a hand to pat the dog, it gave a surprisingly low growl, pulled back its upper lip, and snapped at him. Only a quick retreat saved the mayor's fingers from being bitten. He nearly fell over but righted himself, looking truly shocked. "Muzlim," said the girl, giving the dog a little shake, "what's wrong with you? The nice man only wanted to pet you." She looked up at the crestfallen mayor. "I'm sorry, Mayor Tobald, I don't know what came over him."

"No, no . . ." muttered Tobald. "Strange indeed. I usually get on so *well* with animals." I had to chuckle. Tobald was a jolly, good enough sort, but seeing the high and mighty get a comeuppance, deserved or not, always tickled me. "I'll, uh, get our ales, Grodoveth," the mayor said, retreating to the safety of the bar. Shortshanks may have been as cranky as Muzlim, but at least the dwarf didn't bite.

Grodoveth remained at Barthelm's table, though I didn't hear either the merchant or his daughter invite him to sit. He placed himself across from Mayella, who drew, I fancied, a bit nearer her father as Grodoveth looked at her and gave his impression of a smile. It struck me as more of a smirk.

Their conversation grew quieter than it had been with the garrulous Tobald, and though I couldn't hear what was said, I assumed that it was displeasing to both Barthelm and his daughter. Mayella smiled uncomfortably at first, then a slight blush colored her cheeks.

Barthelm's reaction was more violent. His stern expression slowly grew so tense that I could see his jaw muscles tremble. Finally he leaned toward Grodoveth and spoke in a low, intense voice. I couldn't hear the exact words, but the sibilants hissed at Grodoveth like angry snakes.

The king's envoy sat back, shrugged, and opened his hands as though he had been misunderstood. Then he gave a gravelly laugh, stood up, nodded in what might have been mock politeness, and rejoined Tobald, who was looking on concerned. I heard the mayor ask Grodoveth what was wrong, but the envoy waved the question away and began drinking his ale.

6

Barthelm looked angry for a long time, and I thought I could see the glimmer of tears in Mayella's lovely eyes, but I wasn't about to go and comfort her. I know a furious father when I see one.

"So what do you think *that* was all about?" I asked the tailor, who seemed to know everything.

"The only thing hotter than Grodoveth's temper," he said, "is his taste for the ladies. And he's not always the most tactful of men."

"I'd think," said the chandler, "that Barthelm would be glad to have one of King Azoun's relatives paying attention to his daughter, especially since the only chap she seems set on is that roofer's lad, Rolf."

"But what if that attention is coarse? And what if that king's relative was related to the king by *marriage*?"

"He's married?" the chandler squeaked.

The tailor nodded sagely. "Grodoveth's wife is one of Azoun's cousins."

"That doesn't seem to stop him," I said, "from making suggestions that make maidens blush and fathers bluster. I assume his position and family ties protect him."

"So far," the tailor said. "Though I've heard tell that some indiscretion on his part was what got him booted out of Suzail. By the king hisself, yet. Now it's just a rumor, but I heard that this drab in a Suzail tavern was—"

The no doubt colorful anecdote was abruptly interrupted by the tavern door banging open and the entrance of none other than Dovo, Aunsible Durn's mighty but moronic assistant. He walked in as though he were the gods' gift to women everywhere instead of a metal bender with a wife and three children. He grinned at the men and eyed the ladies saucily, and even had the gall to give a big wink to Mayor Tobald, as though they were on the same social level. The mayor looked as angry as his cheerful countenance allowed, and turned his attention back to his ale and Grodoveth.

Dovo bellied up to the bar, ordered a mug of North Brew, and fell into conversation with a few other town rowdies. I noticed, however, that he was not immune to Mayella's charms, and kept glancing at her as he weaved for his chums some tale of amorous conquest or bullyish retribution. At one point he showed them some small pictures, and from the salacious snickers I assumed they were not miniatures of his kiddies.

After the barmaid, Sunfirth, brought bread and cheese to Barthelm's table, the old man got up and went to use the necessary room. Dovo didn't waste a moment. He whirled around and plunked himself down right across from a startled Mayella, whose little dog was so scared by Dovo's sudden appearance that he hopped up and lay shivering in the girl's lap.

"Ah," breathed Dovo, "there's a lucky little dog. So how are ya this evening, milady? Waitin' for Dovo here to look your way?"

"No sir, I was not."

"Come on now, a course you were!" And so the conversation went for a minute, until the door opened again, letting in a cool autumn breeze and three roofers, hot and tired after a long day's work. At their stern was Rolf, who was in the midst of saying, "Ghost my britches! It's just some boyo having fun, making fools out of everybody. Why, I've half a mind to go out to the Vast Swamp myself and—"

But he stopped when he saw the less than encouraging spectacle before him. Rolf had set his cap for Mayella ever since they were children, and as far as I knew, she had returned his affection, though old Dad had his sights set a mite higher for his daughter.

Rolf was a fairly touchy lad to start with, and when he saw Dovo, the local married lecher, seated across from his beloved, he started shaking as though he wanted to leap on Dovo and rend him limb from limb. But instead he went up behind the smith and laid a heavy hand on his shoulder.

Dovo slowly looked at the hand, then up at the face of its owner. "Well well," he said. "Look who 'tis—Mister Out-In-The-Sun-So-His-Brains-Fry. Go away, little boy. I nearly got this lass talked into a little love walk, and you're liable to queer my play."

That was all it took. With a groan of fury, Rolf yanked his rival backward, tipping his chair over so that it fell with a crash. Dovo's foot caught the table and pulled that on top of him as well, and Rolf followed with a heedless dive into the whole mess.

Bread, cheese, ale, dishes, mugs, and flesh merged together on the floor as the two men, locked in a ferocious struggle, rolled back and forth, knocking the legs out from under Shortshanks's patrons, and tumbling many to the ground. The dwarf came from behind the bar with his twenty-pound oak mallet, a toy with which he had settled many a tavern altercation. But just as he raised it to strike whichever of the two brawlers first came into range, the roar of a single voice froze everyone, including the horizontal combatants.

"STOP!" the voice cried, and when I looked away from the battlers, I saw that Barthelm, who had fathomed everything at a glance, had returned. His was a voice that commanded attention, and Rolf and Dovo looked up for all the world like two mischievous acolytes caught squabbling by their priest. Neither one had a bloody face, though both were coated with ale and bits of cheese and bread.

"Mayella!" Barthelm growled. "Come with me, girl!" She scooted to her father's side, holding the terrified dog under one arm. He took his daughter's hand and led her outside, sharply pulling the door shut behind him as if to seal in the scum.

In the silence, all of us scum bits looked at each other uncomfortably until Shortshanks broke the silence. "Who started it, then? Come on, who was it?" he said, brandishing his mallet.

An angry dwarf with a mallet is a power not to be ignored, and more than a few patrons who had seen it all were soon mumbling, ". . . uh, Rolf . . . Rolf started it . . . yeh, Rolf did it . . . ." and other such comments.

With his free hand Shortshanks grasped Rolf by the ear and pulled on it until the roofer was standing up, though bent over at the waist, for the dwarf still held his ear. "Out with you," Shortshanks said, and with no more explanation than that he led Rolf to the door, yanked it open, and twisted Rolf's ear like he was cracking a whip, so that the lad was flung outside.

Shortshanks slammed the door shut and swung round, glowering at his clientele. "No more trouble tonight," he said, "from anybody." His words were not loud, but we all decided to follow the command implicitly.

The first to speak was Dovo, who was brushing himself off. "I thank you for your wise justice, brother Shortshanks, and to show my appreciation, I should like to buy a drink for all here!" Shortshanks's eyebrows went up, as close to a smile as he got. Then Dovo added, "Although I don't know how so many people are going to get more than a few drops of a single drink. . . ." and started laughing. Shortshanks frowned again, and he curtly ordered Sunfirth to clean up the mess and charge it to Rolf's account.

The girl did as she was told, and recorded the damages in the large account book kept just behind the bar. I felt sorry for her, having to clean up after idiots every night. And speaking of idiots, Dovo remained on the scene, wiping the mess off himself with a bar towel, assuming, no doubt, that his wife would get his clothes clean.

I sat for another half hour, chatting and listening to the drivel that passes for conversation among those slowly getting drunk. Now and then I fancied that I was the great Camber Fosrick, sitting disguised as a wizard's servant in some back-alley watering hole where the vermin of crime met to hatch their dastardly plots. Such a fantasy was difficult to maintain, what with the talk of barley yields and rainfall (or lack thereof), but it got me through the dull patches.

And I was glad I lingered, for at about nine o'clock, in through the door walked one of the most prime specimens of womanhood that I have ever seen.

7

Her perfect if stern face was framed by red hair, cropped off just beneath the woman's chin, leaving her neck bare. She wore a broadbelt that supported a steel bustier, mail leggings, and a leather skirt that was open in front almost to her generous hips.

From the broadbelt hung an assortment of bladed weapons, all of which legally bore peacestrings upon their hilt, though I suspected these symbols of nonaggression would not have prevented the woman from drawing any of her blades efficiently. Although the armor and weaponry was daunting, they did not manage to hide a glorious face and, shall we say, a healthy body that now positioned itself at the dark end of the bar.

"Who," I asked the all-knowing tailor, "is *that*?"

"Must be Kendra," he said quietly. "An adventuress." I had heard of her. But her reputation, though impressive, had not nearly done her justice. "Heard she was coming to the Vast Swamp," the tailor went on. "Supposed to be looking for treasure there."

Her looks alone were treasure enough for a hundred men, I thought, but I kept my opinion to myself. Others were not so tactful. It came as no surprise to me when Dovo lumbered up to Kendra and sat down next to the woman. "Buy you an ale, missy?"

I hope I'm never looked at that coldly by a woman. If Dovo had been any other man, his blood would have frozen, and once it thawed he'd have been on his merry way. But his skull was as thick as his muscles, and he merely leered in response to her sneer. "And what are you?" she said, examining his stained clothing. "Slop boy?"

He colored then, and drew himself up. "Slop boy, is it? Not hardly, missy!"

"Nay indeed!" shouted a tavern wag, safely from a dark corner. "A nail gatherer!"

"A fire stoker!" cried another, given the anonymity of the mob and the tavern's darkness.

"A smith!" insisted Dovo.

"A smith's *assistant*!" cried the first voice.

"Then," said Kendra with a voice that would have frosted over Anauroch, "I'll know who to come to when I want my horse's spit licked off its bridle."

It wasn't the most eloquent insult I'd ever heard, but it got under Dovo's skin. "Watch yourself, missy!" he said loud enough for everyone to hear. "There's more to me than you might think—*much* more."

Kendra glanced down, then looked away disinterestedly. "I doubt it."

He grabbed her arm then and started to whirl her about, but as quick as a snake she pulled out a dagger and pressed it against his throat. "I don't like being touched," she said. "Especially not by a smith's assistant. Barkeep!" she said to Shortshanks. "Why don't you toss this bat's dropping out of your establishment?"

Shortshanks had already come up with that idea on his own. He laid a smart rap behind Dovo's knee with his mallet, and the man nearly fell. "Out!" the dwarf bellowed, and Kendra added to the command by flinging Dovo toward the door.

Dovo went, but with no good grace. He spat on Shortshanks's floor (another cleanup job for poor Sunfirth, thought I) and snarled at Kendra. "No woman treats me like that! I'll show you yet, you—" I shan't say what word he used, but it had Kendra off her stool with a savageness that spurred Dovo to a fast sprint through the door and away into the darkness. The adventuress looked after him for a moment, then returned to the bar without another word.

One would think that such a strong reaction to Dovo's *faux pas* would have taught a lesson to the other men in the Bold Bard. But such was not the case. Mayor Tobald left shortly after the contretemps, with many a yawn and a belch, but Grodoveth remained behind, with a predator's eye on Kendra, who continued to nurse a single mug of Old One Eye.

At last the king's envoy got up and walked over to the beautiful adventuress. Everyone in the tavern suddenly quieted and paid attention, but Grodoveth was using the technique he had used with Mayella— soft and subtle, though not subtle enough for Barthelm's tastes. Not enough for Kendra's either, for she looked at Grodoveth as though he had just fouled her beer, and placed a hand on her sword hilt.

I saw Grodoveth's shoulders shake with a chuckle, and Kendra's expression change from sneer to snarl, showing pearly, perfect teeth. Grodoveth shrugged, said something else that infuriated the woman, then slowly stood up and bowed deeply.

Kendra knew better than to attack an envoy of the king of the land in which she was a guest, and Grodoveth knew she knew it. I can only guess at what he said to her, and those who were close enough to hear would not repeat the words. "Nay," said Tim Butterworth later, "that language I'd not use before the foulest drab in Huddagh."

Grodoveth spoke again, and this time Kendra turned her back on him, wishing, no doubt, that he would grab her as Dovo did, so that she could split his head to the gullet legally. But Grodoveth didn't touch her, just laughed and walked out of the tavern. No one talked to the woman after that but Shortshanks, who apologized for the crude behavior of his customers.

In another half hour I decided to leave as well and return to Benelaius's cottage. He would still be awake. Indeed, I hardly ever saw my master sleeping, in spite of his physical indolence. Perhaps, I thought, his lack of motion made it unnecessary for sleep to refresh him, since he never really expended any energy other than mental.

I retrieved the cask of clarry from behind the bar, settled my account with Shortshanks, and strapped the cask behind the saddle. Then I mounted Jenkus and headed southeast toward the Vast Swamp. *And* the ghost.

* * * * *

I had not had very much to drink, so it was difficult to forget about the stories of Fastred's ghost. I tried to occupy my mind by recalling as best I could everything that had been said and done tonight at the Bold Bard, for I knew Benelaius would want to hear every detail.

He revelled in the stories I brought back from town, and I often wondered why he did not go in himself on occasion. In spite of his corpulence, he was certainly mobile enough, for I once saw him dash across the room to keep an armillary sphere from crashing to the floor after one of the cats had bumped it.

Still, as I drew nearer the Vast Swamp, my mind was filled with the tales of haunts and phantoms and geists, let alone the monsters that I was positive really *did* live in the swamp. I tried to imagine once more that I was the brave and gallant Camber Fosrick, who would laugh at ghosts and snicker at specters.

But by the time I arrived at the fork in the road and turned left toward Benelaius's abode, I was, I confess it, aquiver with nervousness. I tried to avert my glance from the swamp now on my right, but my gaze kept moving there. The moon provided but little light, and I thought that a mercy as I rode on. Jenkus sensed my nervousness, for he was a mite skittish himself, and I kept a firm grasp on his reins.

Then, at a spot where the road curved to bring my path close to the treacherous Vast Swamp, I heard a dull moan, like the voice of a man with his head in a well. It came from the direction of the swamp, and although I told myself to ride on and not to look, of course my head shifted until I was gazing through ribbons of mist. Not twenty yards ahead, so close to the road that it could have reached out and touched me as I passed, I saw what could only be Fastred's ghost.

Naturally I didn't pass. I retained enough presence of mind to haul back manfully on the reins, but Jenkus had anticipated me. Already he had stopped and was backing away from the apparition, and I didn't blame him one bit.

At the sight of the ghost's green and glowing face glaring at me from within an antique helm, my blood had turned to ice in my veins, my stomach felt as though a ten-pound weight of frozen lead had been dropped into it, and my throat felt thick with lard. I couldn't swallow, couldn't speak or even squeak. I have never been so completely terrified.

And when the axe came up, its blade catching the faint rays of moonlight that filtered down through the mist, it got worse.

8

Both Jenkus and I panicked. He reared as I pulled back on the reins so hard we almost toppled over. We wheeled around as though man and horse were one, and dashed as fast as Jenkus could run in the opposite direction. Neither one of us cared where we went, just so long as it was away from that dreadful apparition. We fairly flew down the swamp road, a quite dangerous stunt in the darkness.

But by the time we came to the fork again, I had calmed enough to think about getting to the first place of habitation I could find, and that was among the farmers on the swamp road to the southwest, rather than take the longer journey into Ghars. So I yanked the reins to the left and down the road we went.

The first farmhouse was a scant quarter mile from the fork, and I pulled Jenkus to a stop by its door, swung off, and hailed the folk within. To them, a fat farmer and his fatter wife, I told the story of what I had seen.

The farmer then told me that was quite a tale, and asked what, besides the hot tea and cake they had already given me, they could do about it. I realized that there was nothing. If we returned with a force of farmers, the ghost would probably be nowhere to be seen, even if the farmers were brave enough to go, which I doubted.

They offered to let me spend the night, but when I thought about it, I decided to brave the ghost again. After all, he had not been able to catch me, and if I saw him I could simply ride away. Besides, there was a bit of laughter in the eyes of the farmer and his wife, and I believe they thought me a hysterical chap who had had one too many at the tavern.

So I thanked them, and rode back toward the place of the haunting. Jenkus was not anxious to take the road toward my master's cottage, but I was able to turn his head, and on we rode.

It was well after midnight by now, and I hoped that whatever Fastred had had to do out there he had done and returned to his ghostly home. But my fears were rekindled when, as soon as we left the fork, I heard something up ahead. I swallowed hard, and gave Jenkus a comforting pat on the neck.

But what I heard was not the previous hollow groan, and I saw with relief, not a ghost, but another rider traveling toward me. At that point I would have been happy to see a highwayman, as long as he did not glow.

I could not make out the figure, but it seemed large and was wearing a heavy cloak and a hat with a wide brim that hid its features. I couldn't even tell if it was a man or a woman, and I could see only that the horse was of some dark color, be it black, chestnut, or gray. Dark is dark in the darkness.

"Good evening!" I hailed, more to hear my own

voice than to greet the rider. But there was no reply. Horse and rider passed by me so quickly and dismissively that I never got a glimpse of the shrouded face. Maybe that was another ghost, I thought to myself. Maybe they're having their annual meeting in Ghars as well.

But I didn't really think it a ghost, since Jenkus hardly reacted to it at all, and I had always heard that animals were sound identifiers of spirits. The rider had been moving quickly, but not as speedily as one would who had just seen an axe-swinging ghost. So I assumed the path ahead was free of haunts for the time being.

And it was. I saw nothing untoward all the way back to Benelaius's, though I don't mind telling you that I jumped at every branch that moved in the wind. I was most nervous, of course, at the place where I had seen the thing before. But everything was peaceful. Nothing moved except myself and Jenkus as I kicked him into greater speed past the haunted spot.

It was very late when we arrived home, but Benelaius had of course been awake and working in his study. He greeted me at the door as I entered with the cask of clarry in my arms. "What kept you?"

I shrugged. "Tavern talk, brawls, and most of all, a ghost."

I was glad to see that I had gotten a reaction from his usual stoic countenance. His eyebrows raised. "A ghost, is it?"

"Yes, I saw him near that boggy bit of land where—"

He held up a hand. "On the way there, or the way back?"

"Why, the way back."

"Then start from the beginning, with the tavern talk. It's been a while since I've heard of the doings in town. You'll get to your ghost anon."

Maybe he had had so many experiences with the supernatural in the past that another sighting of a spook had little in it to interest him. But I suspect he told me to offer my tale in chronological order to tease me. I hate being teased.

But he was my master—for another three days— and I did as he asked. We sat in front of the dying fire, and I told him about Barthelm and Mayella Meadowbrock's repast being interrupted by Grodoveth, Mayor Tobald's guest, and what the tailor had told me about the man.

Benelaius nodded sagely. "Yes. I know of the envoy. He was doing quite nicely for himself in Suzail, having married King Azoun's cousin Beatrice, when he dishonored himself and embarrassed the throne by an idiotic act of casual wantonness. His 'reward' was to ride from one small town to another, with that blustering Sarp Redbeard as his supervisor. Very demeaning. Quite a comedown for a man with an ego so huge."

"What, um, *was* the 'act of casual wantonness'?" I asked.

"Nothing for you to be concerned about. Then what happened?"

I told him about Shortshanks's fury over the Swamp Rat, Tobald's little altercation with Mayella's dog, Dovo and Rolf's battle over Mayella, the subsequent departure of the Meadowbrocks, and Grodoveth's unsuccessful attempt at romance with Kendra—in short, all those little events that make small-town life so interesting.

At last, I concluded, "And then, of course, I saw Fastred's ghost, and that's the evening in a nutshell." I stood, stretched, and yawned. "Well, good night, master."

"Good night, Jasper," the wizard said, putting his head back in his easy chair and closing his eyes.

My bluff had not worked. "Master?" I said.

"Mmm?"

"Don't you want to hear about the ghost?"

He opened one eye. "If you wish to tell me." For Benelaius, opening that eye would be akin to you or me jumping up and down in anticipation.

So I told him of the ghost, of my flight, of my visit to the farmer ("that would be Pygmont Kardath," Benelaius said), and of my meeting with the stranger but no further ghosts on the way home.

"Well well well," he said when I had concluded. "It's been quite a full evening for you, Jasper. I suggest you get to bed on the instant, for you must be up at dawn to go into Ghars and meet Lindavar. His coach travels through the night, and should arrive at half past the hour of seven. Sleep well."

I crawled up the dark stairs, circumnavigating the cats sleeping on nearly every one. All of them, that is, save for Razor, who was well named. A coal black cat with yellow eyes, he was notoriously testy, and when I trod, quite by accident, on the end of his tail, he erupted into a spitting, clawing, biting tornado. His fangs sank deeply into my ankle, and with that final *bon mot* he scurried down the stairs to seek a less hazardous berth.

I barely managed to restrain a painful scream, but I made my way to my room, put a poultice on the wound, and quickly fell into an exhausted sleep, disturbed frequently by dreams of giant black cats spitting fire, glowing green, and swinging axes whose blades were rows of fangs. I'd far rather have dreamed of Mayella or Kendra or even Sunfirth, but no. I had to dream about cats with axes.

9

The morning came faster than a werejaguar with a fire under it. My ankle ached, my eyes were stuck shut with sleep sand, and my stomach was queasy, I feared, from Shortshanks's cod pie.

But when you're a servant you don't let little things like that get in the way of your duty. After a quick breakfast of a poached egg on blackbread, I hitched the two horses to the carriage and started off for Ghars. Stubbins fell in quickly enough, but Jenkus was quite put out about being made to work so soon after his service of the night before. Me, too, for all the good it did us.

Actually, it almost felt like the night before. The sun had not yet come over the horizon, but its light bathed the landscape in a pinkish glow. As the carriage rattled along, the egg and bread in my stomach churned a bit. My stomach wasn't helped by the fact that Jenkus's reluctance to pull kept getting the coach off course, requiring a firm hand on the reins.

At last Jenkus seemed to accept his fate, and we went on a relatively straight path toward Ghars.

As we passed the spot where I had seen the apparition, I tried to avert my eyes, which wasn't too difficult, since they were closed in half-sleep for most of the ride. But I thought that from the corner of my eye I glimpsed a shape on the ground, out near the swamp, and a dull sheen on it not found in nature.

Did I conquer my fears of seeing a hideous wight or zombie or meazel or even a gibbering mouther rise up out of the swamp to capture and devour me? Did I turn and look fully into what I prayed was only a mound of swamp muck with a wet sheen?

I did not. I buried my head down into my cloak like the coward I sometimes am, and shook the reins in the fruitless hope that Stubbins and Jenkus would increase their speed.

But nothing came after me, and a ways down the road I turned and looked back uneasily, half expecting to be pounced upon from behind by some stealthy pursuer. The mound was discernible, far back in the distance, and the rising sun glinted off something. But now was not the time for investigation. On the way back would be best, in the company of a War Wizard with a good many combat spells at his disposal.

That War Wizard, however, turned out to be a pretty unassuming sort. He was sitting on a bench outside the Sheaf of Wheat, his nose in a book and several small satchels at his feet. He wore a slouch hat, and a dusty brown cloak covered his thin body. When he stood, I could see that he was of only medium height, though half a head taller than me.

"Sir, are you Lindavar, the wizard Benelaius's guest?"

He looked as though he had to think about it for a

minute, but answered, "Uh, yes . . . yes I am."

I introduced myself and started to load his bags into the carriage. He began to help, but I said, "Oh, no, sir. Please rest yourself. I'll be happy to take care of everything." I can lie perfectly when I have to. It's a talent that everyone in service needs to have, along with a strong back and little need for sleep.

Then he started to climb up front with me, until I told him that he would sit more comfortably in the back. He demurred so delicately that he reminded me of a polite child. "But I should see ever so much better up here."

I shrugged. "Very well then, sir, wherever you wish." I didn't know what he would find so visually appealing. The land southeast of Ghars is just farms and swamp, but he was the boss.

He spoke nary a word on the first part of the journey, and I respected the silence, like a good servant. Now and then he'd ask me what bird had just flown past, or what crop was growing in that field.

I was telling him as much as I knew about farming oats, which was minimal, when he suddenly stiffened. "What is that up there?" he asked.

For a moment I thought he had seen the ghost again, and my heart leapt into my throat. But then I saw the mound I had detected only briefly on the way. It was perhaps fifty feet off the road, nearly at the edge of the swamp itself, and now that I gathered the courage to look at it dead on (apt words!), it looked like nothing more nor less than a body clad in armor.

"Do you see it?" Lindavar asked me, and I nodded dully. When we were close to it, the wizard told me to stop the carriage. "It looks like someone lying out there," he said, alarm in his voice, and stepped off the road onto the marshy earth at the swamp's edge.

"Sir, be careful!" I said. "The swamp could pull you down if you don't watch your step!"

If he heard me, he ignored me, and kept walking toward the figure, heedless of the mud that sucked at his boots. Like a good and idiotic servant, I followed him.

"Sir, I might add that only yesternight I saw a terrible specter clad in armor right at this spot. It could be a monster of some sort, sir, playing possum to draw you closer. Sir? Did you hear me, sir?"

"It's no monster," he called back. "It looks like a man!"

I wasn't so sure. It looked to me as though it was wearing the same armor that I had seen garbing my ghost. "Sir, I beg you, as you must know from your calling, such creatures have the power to put on a piteous shape, and then leap up and grasp their would-be helper. It may not be a man at all!"

It was too late. Lindavar was already kneeling by the side of what I was convinced was a malingering ghost, and I expected at any second to see a pair of taloned hands come up and rend him to bits. But instead he straightened up, holding a large metal helmet on its side. It was the same one that I had seen Fastred's ghost wearing the night before. He turned toward me and held out the helmet, from the base of which dripped a reddish muck.

Then he opened the closed visor, and I realized that the head was still in it.

"Is it not a man?" said Lindavar in grim confirmation.

A familiar face, now a sickly green, stared with bulging eyes through the opening of the visor. "It is," I whispered.

"Dovo."

10

"You know him?" asked Lindavar, coming closer with his dread burden.

I backed away. Maybe wizards are used to lugging around dead body parts, but it wasn't my cup of tea. "Yes, I know . . . *knew* him. Look, would you please put that down?" My egg and blackbread were really churning now that I saw the reddish muck wasn't merely swamp ooze.

Lindavar started to set down the helmeted head, but it tilted and the head slid right out the bottom of the helmet. It made a wet plop as it hit the swampy ground. "Ooogh," I muttered, and looked away.

"Who was he?" Lindavar asked.

"His name was Dovo. He was the smithy's assistant in Ghars." I considered not speaking ill of the dead, then dismissed it. After all, Dovo had played a pretty rotten trick on me last night, and on a lot of people by the looks of it. "He was a dolt."

Lindavar looked down at the head thoughtfully.

"Why do you say that?"

"Because he's been dressing up like a ghost and scaring people. I saw him last night. He was wearing that armor. . . ."I pointed at the headless body lying arms akimbo. A pool of blood had thickened into a brown-black custard at the corpse's neck. "That's probably luminous paint on his face. . . ."I nodded at the pale green color of Dovo's skin. "And he was carrying that axe," I finished quietly. That particular implement was lying near the body, its long curved blade dark with dried blood.

"How far is Benelaius's cottage?" asked Lindavar. I thought it an abrupt change of topic.

"Another mile up this road," I answered.

"Very well. You stay here, Jasper, and I'll go and fetch him."

The hairs on the back of my neck tickled. "What? Me stay here? Why?"

"Because there should be someone at the scene of the crime. If no one's here, someone else could come along and disturb the evidence, or beasts could come out of the swamp and devour the body, or the killer could return."

"And if the beasts or the killer comes, what am I supposed to do about it?" I knew that as a good servant I shouldn't question an order, but this one made me a touch edgy.

"If the killer comes back," said Lindavar, "you can hide and see who it is, and if any beasts come . . . well, I shouldn't be gone that long."

"But—"

"Now, Jasper, as a great man once said, 'A brave and steadfast heart can overcome any fear.' So don't worry. I'll be back with Benelaius shortly. In the meantime, look about for clues, only don't disturb anything."

And without another howdydo, he trotted back to the road, hopped up onto the carriage, and set the horses toward Benelaius's.

I knew only too well who that great man was whom he spoke of. Camber Fosrick. I had committed the quote to memory as well. So Lindavar, one of the War Wizards of Cormyr, was addicted to trashy literature too. I would have chuckled had I not been so scared.

So I thought about Fosrick's quote and came to the conclusion that, although I greatly admired the detective, it was poppycock. What it said was, that if you were brave, then you would be brave. It didn't tell you how to get that way. Cold comfort indeed, I can tell you.

I decided to follow Lindavar's other piece of advice and use the time searching for clues. That would keep my mind off beasts and killers, and the investigation would be that much further along by the time Benelaius arrived.

So with great care I began to walk all around the corpse, being careful not to step on footprints. The sodden ground had held those of Lindavar and myself well, but earlier prints had nearly disappeared, the swamp pushing up against the indentations as if to deny that man had ever trod there. The few marks that were left appeared to have been made by someone with big feet, and I looked at the soles of Dovo's corpse. They were big all right, like everything else on the man.

Since all the footprints were big, I figured that the feet of the killer had to be large also. All right, then, the killer had big feet. I felt Camber Fosrick would be proud of me, brave or not. Also, none of the footprints led farther toward the swamp, so whoever beheaded Dovo must have come from the road and left that way. Another brilliant deduction, I thought. Unless the killer flew, but the odds of that seemed long.

Then I searched the ground for things smaller than footprints, and found a few. The severed tips of three fingers lay closely together, and I shuddered as I glanced at Dovo's corpse. The right hand was visible, with all its digits intact, but the left hand was covered by the corpse. I didn't move it to look for stumps.

There were also some small shards of broken glass several feet away from Dovo's body. I left them where they were, but I could see that they were clear rather than colored, and slightly curved as well.

The costume of the corpse was far less impressive than I had thought it the night before. I would have sworn, for instance, that my ghost had been wearing a full suit of gleaming armor, and a helmet with a crest that made the whole ensemble over twelve feet tall.

But the light of day showed only a worn breast-plate, tarnished where it wasn't dented, and mail leggings whose links had come loose in a dozen places. The helmet was small and squat, and had no plume at all. Only the axe was an impressive piece of metal, its blade curving a full two feet along its edge.

Dovo's head was lying faceup, his wide eyes staring sightlessly at a blue Cormyrean sky. I summoned the courage to go closer to it and, using a leaf, wiped some of the green covering from the flesh. Then I held the leaf in one hand and made a circle with the other, peering into it. The green stuff glowed dimly, even with the sunlight pushing between my fingers. It was luminous, all right. The effect had been ghastly in last night's darkness.

Now I walked up to the road to look for any clues, scanning the ground on the way. The road, though dry, was a confusion of hoofprints and cart tracks, and I could make nothing of them. Then I sat by the side of the road and waited, the farther from the corpse and the swamp the better.

I don't know how long I sat there, but the sun was far up in the sky by the time someone came. And then it was like a party. Down the western road rode five horsemen, and much closer, rounding a bend from the east, Benelaius's carriage approached. I could see Lindavar driving, and from the close proximity of the bottom of the carriage to the road, I could tell that my corpulent master was inside. At least now I knew what it would take to get him out of his house—a murder.

When the carriage pulled up next to me, the horsemen were still a few minutes away. I opened the door for Benelaius and, forgetting my station as I so often do, said, "What took you so long . . . master?"

He clucked at me patiently. "As you know, Jasper, I do not get out very often. I felt I should look my best."

And so he did. His hair and long gray beard were neatly combed, and he wore a stylish, hooded dress cloak that I had not known he possessed, and a pair of nearly new high kid boots, instead of his usual fuzzy wool slippers.

He looked past me at the horsemen. "I see the authorities have arrived as well. Good. The more heads the better, even if some of them are a mite thickish."

Now the riders were close enough for me to see who they were. In the lead was Captain Flim, the head of Ghars's garrison of Purple Dragons, with two other Dragons flanking him. One of them led an empty mount that would, I assumed, bear Dovo's body back to Ghars.

Behind the Dragons was Mayor Tobald, who looked as if he was having difficulty staying in the saddle, and the equally talkative Doctor Braum.

I turned back to Benelaius in surprise. "They know about the murder?"

He nodded. "As soon as Lindavar told me, I sent the bird." He meant the carrier dove that sat in a hanging cage in his study. I'd never known him to use it before. He spoke to it at times, but he always let me think it was a pet. It was interesting to see that it had a talent other than extraordinary equanimity in the presence of dozens of cats. "In the message, I said only that Dovo had been killed, and that we suspected foul play." Then Benelaius turned toward the party that came riding up. "Greetings, gentlemen," he said.

"Is it true?" Tobald asked my master as he nearly tumbled off his steed. "Is it Dovo?"

Benelaius acknowledged me, and I nodded. "He's down there by the swamp," I said. "His head's been cut off."

It was hardly an apropos time for Benelaius to introduce Lindavar, but Captain Flim was looking at him curiously, so my master graciously did the honors. Then we went down to the body.

At the grisly sight of it, they acted the way I had expected. Flim and his Dragons' attitude was that they had seen it all before (and they had); Doctor Braum was appalled by the sight but tried to act clinical; and Mayor Tobald seemed just plain shocked, finally at a loss for words. In fact, he had a little trouble keeping his breakfast down.

As Benelaius observed the corpse, however, he acted as though he were examining a new and interesting kind of bug rather than a dead smith.

"Why, uh . . ." Tobald said, belching and frowning at the taste, "why is he wearing that armor?"

"My servant Jasper can answer that," said Benelaius.

I nodded. "It was part of his trick, his impersonation."

"Jasper saw the ghost last night," Benelaius said. "Fastred's ghost, or so he thought. Something dressed in old armor and helmet, with an axe and a glowing green face. Care to draw any quick conclusions?"

"You mean," Flim said slowly, as if trying to work out what letter comes after *A*, "this man was playing at being the ghost?"

"Apparently," said Benelaius. "And his bogus appearance answers the description given by most of those who have seen the so-called haunt. I think you'll find that unguent on his face . . . the green that's *not* mold . . . is derived from glimmergrass."

"Now wait a moment, Benelaius," Tobald said briskly. He seemed to have once more become his old garrulous self. "Are you saying that when I saw the ghost, it was Dovo I saw?"

"I believe so."

Tobald shook his head firmly. "My friend, I have no doubt that I can tell the difference between a real apparition and an imposter such as this!"

Benelaius began to shrug, but since his body was not made for shrugging, he abandoned the effort. "Perhaps you did, Tobald. I know for a fact that ghosts exist, as do spirits capable of doing . . . what was done to Dovo here."

Tobald's face was as one who suddenly finds enlightenment. "That must be it, then! This"—he gestured to the corpse, then looked quickly away, swallowing hard—"this is supernatural vengeance. Fastred's ghost has taken his revenge on the human who mocked him!"

"Maybe . . . or *maybe not*," said Benelaius in a tone that told me he was on the maybe not side. "Tell me,

Jasper, did you find any footprints other than your own, Lindavar's, and Dovo's?"

"Well, sir, as best I was able to make out, there were two people here, both with big feet. And Dovo had big feet."

"Are you sure," said the doctor, "that they weren't just one set of big feet? I tend to favor Tobald's theory."

"As might I," said Benelaius, "save for three things. The first is the extra set of footprints—I have more faith in Jasper's evidence-gathering skills than you, you see. Here is the second." He pointed a pudgy finger at the axe. "This is certainly the murder weapon, caked with Dovo's blood. Why would not the ghost of Fastred use his own axe? And if he had lost it somewhere over in the spirit world, why would he not take this one along?" He smiled. "It certainly seems sharp enough.

"As for the third thing, beside a few severed fingers, I note the presence of several small shards—"

"Of clear glass!" I volunteered, wanting them to know that I had seen the clues, too.

"Very good, Jasper," said Benelaius with a trace of sarcasm that only I would have noticed. "And your conclusion?"

"Um . . . something broke?"

"Yes. But what?"

"Something . . . made of glass . . ." I suspect Captain Flim would have done as well as I.

"The glass is curved, is it not?" said my master. "And what is partially made of curved glass that a human might require out in a pitch-black swamp?"

"A lantern!" This from Doctor Braum, just before I was about to say it.

"Correct," said Benelaius. "This glass, if I'm not mistaken, is part of a broken panel from the metal housing of a bullseye lantern."

"So Dovo had a lantern out here," said Tobald. "He'd need one in the dark. So how does that prove that Fastred's ghost was not involved?"

Benelaius looked about the ground eloquently. I saw what he meant. "It proves it right enough," said I. "The lantern's gone. But what need would a ghost have for a lantern? And a broken one at that? Someone human did this deed."

"And you, Jasper," said Benelaius, "have seen him, from mere feet away."

11

Well, *that* stopped everybody dead in their tracks. They all turned and looked at me in amazed expectation, except for Captain Flim and his men, who were still in their uninvolved professionals mode.

At first my mind was a blank, and then it hit me. "The rider," I said. "The rider I passed last night."

"You see," Benelaius explained, "after Jasper saw Dovo as the ghost last night, he . . . retreated down the road to the west, alerted a farmer, had a wee stay with him, and then returned. Between this spot and the road to Ghars, he met . . . ?"

"A . . . a man . . . I think, riding a dark horse."

"Did you see him?" asked Tobald.

"No . . . I mean, I don't even know if it *was* a man. It could have been anyone. The person was all bundled up."

"And what time was this?" asked Doctor Braum.

"Between midnight and one."

"How long has Dovo been dead, doctor?" said

Benelaius. "Your best estimate."

Doctor Braum knelt by the corpse, muttering. "Easier to say when the head's attached . . ." He pressed the dead flesh, then rolled the body over. All of us gasped—even Flim and his Dragons gave a quick breath—when we saw Dovo's mutilated hand. "There's where those fingers came from, Benelaius," said Braum, "as if we couldn't have guessed." Braum poked and prodded a little more, then said, "Roughly, between ten and twelve hours."

"That fits," I said. "That rider could have been the killer." I felt suddenly faint as I realized how close I might have come to death. What had there been to prevent the killer from hewing me in two as well, except, of course, that he had left the axe with his victim? I would have sat down had there been any place where my buttocks wouldn't have sunk into muck.

"Think, Jasper," Tobald urged. "Wasn't there anything about this person you can recall? Was it a skilled or an unskilled rider? Did they sit as if they were dwarven or elven or human? Male or female? Can't you recall even that? Man or woman?"

As if destined, a hail came from up on the road. We turned to look and saw the womanly vision that had entered the Bold Bard the previous night. Kendra was straddling a dark gray horse. A heavy hooded cloak enveloped her completely, so that, had I not seen her face, I could not have told whether she was a male or a female rider.

That thought at that time gave me pause. But I did see her face, framed by that halo of red hair, and it looked down with cold eyes on the scene of slaughter. She dismounted with the grace of one born in the saddle, adjusted her cloak so that the hilts of her weapons preceded her, and walked toward our merry band.

When she was close enough to see the features on the face of the severed head, she examined it appraisingly, looked at the axe and the torso in armor, and then nodded. "I see that fool at the tavern last night has been even more foolish. So this is the ghost that's been haunting the Vast Swamp, eh? It seems someone wasn't amused by the joke."

She had put it together quickly, too quickly for Captain Flim's taste. "How did you know he was posing as the ghost?"

She gave a half-laugh. "It's obvious, isn't it? Even to a Purple Dragon captain."

The comment did not endear her to Flim. "You're Kendra, aren't you? I've heard about you. You're the adventuress who held a dagger to this lad's throat last night!"

"Aye," she answered, "and would have used it, too, and gladly." She glared back down at both parts of the corpse. "He was a pig and a fool, and I for one am not sorry to see such men die."

"Nor would you be sorry to kill them?" Captain Flim said.

"A knife's my weapon, Captain, not an axe."

"So where were you last night after you left the tavern?"

She looked at Flim indignantly. "Are you accusing me, Captain? Do you wish to arrest me?"

"I'm just asking, *madam!*"

"Very well then, I'll tell you. I left the tavern after only a few drinks, rode my horse to a place south of town, and there, among a copse of trees, I slept through the night."

"And then?" pursued the captain.

"I got up."

"To what purpose?"

"To the purpose of adventuring. That's what I do.

You're a soldier, you soldier. I'm an adventuress, I adventure. Whee."

I glanced at Benelaius to see if he might try to direct the conversation more efficiently, but he was merely smiling and seeming to enjoy the exchange. That's what comes of not getting out more.

"Then where are you bound now?" said Captain Flim.

"To the Vast Swamp. If you must know, I'm looking for Fastred's treasure. I know, it's only a legend, but I've often found that legends have their bases in truth."

"You're mighty late starting out," Flim said, cocking his head and peering at her through his Purple Dragons' headgear. "Most adventurers would have started out far earlier than you. Something keep you up last night?"

"No, something kept me down this morning—a ride all the way from Wheloon yesterday and an encounter with two thieves on the way, which I wouldn't have had to deal with if the military of this country took its job more seriously."

That smarted. Flim nearly staggered back as if struck. Then he composed himself and asked, "Where were these highwaymen? I shall send a squadron after them immediately!"

"Never mind, they're both dead. Sorry I had to break your little peacestring rule, but I didn't have a choice. Now, any more questions?"

"Where will we be able to reach you?" Flim said officiously.

Kendra smiled and made a sweeping gesture toward the swamp. "In there. I'll stop back in Ghars when I come out. If I don't come out, well"—she looked at me and recognized me from the tavern—"raise a glass to me, will you?"

"Gladly, madam," I said. "Go well."

She turned around, the hem of her cloak billowing and catching the captain's shins. He winced, and I knew then the hem was lined with orc spikes. Clever girl. The captain said nothing, however. Brave lad.

We watched her walk back to her horse, and even her manly garb could not disguise the sensuous motion beneath.

"Quite a woman," said Lindavar.

"Yes indeed," Benelaius agreed. "Although she has the largest pair of feet I've ever seen on a female. Perhaps that's how she holds her stirrups so well."

12

I must confess that the last place I had looked on Kendra's dramatic form was her feet. But as I glanced down at the tracks she had left in the soft ground, I saw that Benelaius was right.

"Could she have been the one you saw last night, Jasper?" Tobald asked me, watching Kendra's departing form.

"She could have been," I said. "She's tall enough. But then so are a hundred other people in Ghars."

"Let's retain her in the backs of our minds," said Benelaius, "and see what else we might find. Doctor Braum, as you examine the body—*and* the head— what do you determine to be the cause of Dovo's death?"

Braum frowned in confusion. "Well, it's difficult to live when your head and body are in two different places."

"Indeed. But how was the fatal blow struck?"

"Hard?" suggested Captain Flim.

"Certainly. But upon what side did it strike the victim? By determining this, we might be able to learn something about the killer."

The light in Braum's eyes turned on. "Ah, I see! The fingers of his left hand are cut off, which means that he probably put up that hand to ward off the blow . . ."

"Fat chance of doing that," Flim said.

"So," said Tobald excitedly, getting in the game, "in all likelihood he was facing his slayer . . . and he was struck on the left side . . . so that means the killer struck with his"—he paused a moment and mimed swinging an axe—"his *right* hand!"

"Yes!" Dr. Braum agreed. "So we must look for a right-handed killer!"

Captain Flim snorted. "Oh, *that* makes it easy. Who am I supposed to be, Camber Fosrick?" It seemed that the captain was yet another fan of the great consulting cogitator.

"It's true, Captain," said Mayor Tobald. "This really isn't much to go on. There were a few people who Dovo had rough words with last night. Rolf, for one."

"And Barthelm Meadowbrock for another," I said. "Not to mention Kendra. And they're not the only ones. I know of a number of people Dovo's offended in some manner. He's cuckolded his share of husbands, I've heard. With all due respect," I said, nodding at the corpse, "he wasn't the most liked fellow in Ghars."

Tobald shrugged. "Well, Captain Flim, I have much to do in preparing for the arrival of the Merchants' Guild council, so I'm going to leave this business in your capable hands. Return the body to town, and please inform the widow. Then begin the search for the perpetrator of this deed."

"Begging your pardon, sir," said Captain Flim, "but

my duty to my garrison must come first. What with the threat of Zhentarim and Iron Throne agents, most of my time is spent overseeing efforts to apprehend them."

"If I might make a suggestion," said Benelaius, "why not let Jasper and Lindavar and I pursue this problem? Under Captain Flim's supervision, of course."

"Sounds good to me." Flim sounded relieved.

"After all," Benelaius went on after nodding his thanks, "I am a former War Wizard, Lindavar is a present one, and Jasper can prove quite valuable as my eyes and ears." Then he smiled at me the way a mother dog smiles at her runt. "Besides, he has read a Camber Fosrick book."

"So be it!" cried Tobald. "And thank you, good Benelaius. I knew that when you came to dwell here you would prove a valuable addition to our community. If I can be of any service, let me know. I hereby make you and your friends honorary magistrates of Ghars, with all of the rights appertaining to that position. Go where you like, and question whomever you wish on my authority."

"I thank *you*, good Mayor Tobald," Benelaius said, I think to shut Tobald up as much as anything. "Lindavar and Jasper and I will return to my home now to discuss our next step."

And that's just what we did, leaving the mayor and the doctor to ride back to Ghars and the Dragons to follow with the dead Dovo. I prepared my master and his guest a tasty luncheon, in which he invited me to share as we discussed the murder.

"Jasper," Benelaius said, "I want you to go to Ghars this afternoon. Use your intuition. Talk to people. See what their reactions are to Dovo's death. Aunsible Durn might be able to shine some light on Dovo's activities. He was, after all, Durn's assistant.

"I suppose there's always a chance that he could have been the victim of highwaymen. The envoy Grodoveth travels more than anyone else in town. If he has not yet departed, you might ask him whether he had seen any suspicious parties in his travels. Also, I wonder what happened to Dovo's outer garments. And his horse, for that matter. He surely didn't walk out there wearing armor.

"So put your ear to the ground, Jasper. Spend another evening at the Bold Bard. Stop at the Swamp Rat on the way home. Pretend you're"—he sighed—"Camber Fosrick. And do try to be back before midnight."

"I'll do my best, sir," I said, though nettled by the Camber Fosrick crack. I didn't know what better role model I could find.

"And even if you learn absolutely nothing," Benelaius concluded, "the trip won't be a total loss." He handed me a huge volume that I had hauled from the tiny Ghars library a few weeks before. "Return this, won't you?"

13

Jenkus was not at all cheerful about the prospect of another ride so soon after his hauling Benelaius's carcass back and forth to the murder site, but he had no more choice than I did. Secretly, I was delighted with the prospect of investigating this murder. There's nothing like a headless corpse to bring a touch of excitement into one's life.

I had, after all, taken quite a step in the past twenty-four hours—from being an errand boy to being a government-licensed criminal investigator. Perhaps, using what Benelaius had already taught me and what I would learn from this experience, I could make it my career when I received my freedom a few days hence.

But my first duty in Ghars was the mundane one of returning Benelaius's book to the library. I glanced at the name on the binding and saw that it was another deadly dull treatise on natural science—*The Internal Structure of the Brachiopod* by Professor Linnaeus

Gozzling of the University of Suzail. Dreadful stuff, but Benelaius gobbled it up by the double handsful.

It was just after four by the time I lumbered into Ghars, plenty of time to return the book before the library closed. The library was just a large room that had been tacked on to the town hall years back. It held a gloomy assortment of material, mostly books over fifty years old, and none of the recent thrillers about Camber Fosrick, else I should have lived there.

No, the place leaned more toward history, which was the particular passion of the librarian, Phelos Marmwitz, whose personal collection made up half the library's holdings. There was also a decent section of natural history, philosophy, and other dry subjects, a smattering of imaginative literature, and drawers filled with dry and crumbling antique maps of Cormyr and environs, many of which were drawn in great detail but were very much out of date.

As I entered the dark, dingy room, the smell of mildew struck me, and as always I feared for those books against the damp outer wall. "Good afternoon, Mr. Marmwitz," I said, but the thin, wizened old man waved his hands in the air and made a hissing noise through his teeth intended to shush me.

"Please, *quiet*," Marmwitz said in a stage whisper with a voice as dry and papery as his books. "We have a patron." And he pointed with a bony hand to a corner near one of the small windows.

A patron *was* a rarity, and I was surprised to see that it was none other than Grodoveth, king's envoy and ladies' man, though not too hot at the latter. He looked up at me for a moment, apparently saw nothing worth further consideration, and plunged back into his reading.

I set the brachiopod book down on the counter. Marmwitz opened it suspiciously, glanced at the due date as though he had expected it back years before, then with a nod acknowledged grudgingly that it was on time. I couldn't resist. "Get anything new in lately?" I asked him.

He gave a proud little smile. "A town history of Juniril," he said. "A splendid volume, published forty years ago. Been looking for it for ages."

"Forty years ago," I mused. "Not too new. Still no Camber Fosrick mysteries, eh?"

His face shut up like a clam sucking lemons. "We circulate only serious literature here, young man."

"Ah, right. I forgot." I turned to go out, when I remembered that Benelaius had asked me to query Grodoveth about seeing any highwaymen. I wouldn't have done it in the library, but I didn't know if I would see the man again, and there was another reason, too.

"Mr. Marmwitz," I said quietly, "I want you to know that I do what I do now at the behest of my master Benelaius and with the authority of Mayor Tobald." Then I turned to Grodoveth, who still had his nose buried in his book. "Sir," I said in a normal tone of voice, which boomed loudly in the quiet room, "I wonder if I might have a word with you."

I thought Marmwitz was going to become apoplectic. I turned back to him. "This will only take a minute, Mr. Marmwitz." Ignoring Marmwitz's stammering protests, I went to Grodoveth's table and sat across from him.

He slammed shut the book he was reading, covered its spine, and glared at me, making me wonder if he had somehow found an erotica section and was annoyed at being discovered. "What is it?" he asked brusquely.

"I was wondering, sir, if you may have heard of the death of one of our residents."

"Who?"

"Dovo. The smith's assistant."

"Why would I have heard about it?"

I shrugged. "I didn't know but that it might be the talk of the town by now. Anyway, sir, he was killed south of town, near the Great Swamp, and my master asked me if—"

"Who's your master?"

"Benelaius, sir. Used to be one of the War Wizards of Cormyr?"

"I've heard of him. What's he want?"

"He wonders if you, in your travels about the realm, might have heard of any bands of brigands who would kill their victims in that manner."

He looked at me slyly. "What manner?"

"Oh, I forgot to say. He was beheaded, sir. With an axe. We think he was pretending to be the ghost that's supposed to haunt the swamp."

"Ghost?"

"Yes, sir, the ghost of Fastred."

"Listen, I don't know anything about any brigands who cut people's heads off, and I couldn't care less about ghosts. Now why don't you get out of here and let me read in peace?"

I could take a hint. Thanking him for his cooperation, I left the library, to Marmwitz's great relief, but I waited outside until Grodoveth left a few minutes later. Then I went back in. I wanted to see what book there could possibly be in Ghars's library that would make someone cover it up.

Mr. Marmwitz was not pleased to see me, but I gave him a friendly grin just the same and went over to where Grodoveth had been sitting. The book was no longer on the table, but since Grodoveth hadn't left with it, it still was there somewhere. He had probably put it back on the shelf, but I thought I'd ask

Marmwitz just the same.

"Sir, your pardon," I said softly, "but as part of my . . . investigation on the behest of Benelaius and Mayor Tobald, I should like to know in what subject area the gentleman who just left was reading."

Marmwitz looked crankier than I ever hoped to get, but he answered. "Local subjects."

"Ah. And does Grodoveth take out many volumes on that subject?"

"He takes out no volumes at all. Only residents of Ghars may withdraw books."

I nodded thoughtfully and went over to the section on local history and folklore. Most of the books were very old, and I saw that my master had copies of a good many of them in his library. Then I realized that I could tell which books had been taken off the shelf because of disturbances in the dust. For all his fussiness, Marmwitz was not a superlative housekeeper.

Nearly a dozen books had been removed and replaced, and I took them all to the table and perused them. Most of them fell open readily enough, as is the case with old and brittle volumes. I supposed Grodoveth had never learned of the proper and gentle care of books, the very first lesson Benelaius taught me. For every one of these volumes opened to a passage or chapter about either the historical or the legendary Fastred.

There was a wealth of information about the brigand, and apparently Grodoveth had read it all. Yet he had said he wasn't interested in ghosts. He was lying about something, that was for sure.

"Mr. Marmwitz," I said, "you don't have a lot of people using the library, do you?"

His instant sorrow showed that I had struck a nerve. "No, and more's the pity. Days go by when no one comes in at all. Mr. Grodoveth has come in occasionally during the past few months, but our daily traffic is tragically minimal."

"That *is* a shame," I said, catching the fly with honey. "This really is a grand repository of information. So when did you say Grodoveth started coming in here?" All right, so I wasn't very good at smooth transitions, but I was still learning.

Marmwitz didn't bat an eye, however. "My, let's see, it must have been, oh, back around Tarsakh or so."

Tarsakh. Five months before. And at least two months before the recent flock of ghost sightings had begun. So why was Grodoveth, the king's envoy, looking into the matter of Fastred's ghost before that ghost, in the person of Dovo, began to make his reappearances?

It didn't make any sense to me. Either Grodoveth could see into the future, or he had something to do with the phony ghost, or it was one amazing coincidence. Maybe, I thought, Benelaius would be able to make some sense out of it.

I thanked Marmwitz and cautioned him not to say anything about my curiosity. Then, before I returned the books to the shelf, I copied down their titles and the page numbers to tell Benelaius. I would have withdrawn them, but I didn't want to start Grodoveth wondering where they had gone if he should return to the library the following day. Odds were that Benelaius owned most of the books anyway.

Next I went over to Aunsible Durn's smithy. The establishment had no name, for it was the only smithy in town. Indeed, a man would have been a fool to have opened a smithy in competition with Durn, for his skill was tremendous, and he was always busy.

The only sign of his trade was what looked like an ever-glowing lump of coal that hung from a curved rod in front of his smithy. It was actually a bumpy globe of red glass inside of which some wandering mage had placed a continual light spell. Durn must have paid the bargain rate, for the light constantly waxed and waned, though it never quite went out.

Durn was too busy to talk at the moment. It was near closing time, and in the absence of his late assistant, Dovo, he had a backlog of work. Besides the horse he was currently shoeing, two other riders waited with their mounts, so that it was nearly seven o'clock when he wearily set down his tools.

I had stayed out of the way all the time, listening to Durn's conversation with his clients, which was minimal. He was a man of few words in the smithy and never once asked me what I was doing there. But when he was away from the anvil, he was among the most garrulous of men.

As the last client led his newly shod horse out of the smithy, Durn finally acknowledged me. "And what do you want, Jasper?"

"A word or two, Aunsible Durn, about Dovo."

Durn shook his head. "I don't know what grieves me more, his death or the fact that I have been without a helper all day long. Come upstairs and have a cup of tea with me."

We climbed the round staircase in the corner of the smithy, up past the second floor lofts where Durn stored his supplies, and stopped on the top floor, a modest apartment where Durn lived alone. As he brewed a tea that reeked strongly of seaweed, I explained my mission to him, and we talked about Dovo.

"He was a good worker, for all his other faults," Durn said. "The gods know I missed him terribly today. Yes, he would be off at the taverns roistering away, but never when there was work to be done. Still, I pity his wife and children. He paid little attention to them when he was alive, and now they shall not even have the comfort of his salary since he is dead. Though perhaps," he added roughly, "I can help in some way."

"You heard he was playing the ghost?"

Durn gave a snort of disgust. "Aye, just like him. Always on the lookout for a prank or a jest. He tried that here the first week he worked for me. Put a burr under his friend Argys Kral's saddle. When Argys mounted, the mare went crazy and threw him off. I let Dovo know in no uncertain terms"—Durn pounded a fist into his palm—"that type of behavior would not be tolerated in my smithy. He never gave me trouble after."

"Did he ever say anything about the ghost to you?"

"He said he saw it. In fact, I believe he was the first one—setting everyone up for his little joke. Must've been, oh, back in Mirtul, four months ago. Told me, and probably everybody in the tavern, that Fastred's ghost had come out at him one night while he was riding home from the Swamp Rat. Said it took a great swing at him with its axe, and showed a cut in his cloak to prove it. Got a lot of mileage out of that story, he did, and made everyone nervous enough that they were ready to see a ghost even without him pretending to be one. Guess somebody didn't think it was very funny."

"True enough," I said. "I know that he was quite a hand with the ladies. Is there anyone you can think of who might have wished him ill?"

"Husbands and suitors, you mean? 'Twould be a long line, I fear. I know little about the details of his romances. That was another thing I told him right off to keep out of the smithy. If his philandering lost me customers, I would let him go. But that never happened." Durn shrugged his heavy shoulders. "People here have little choice. They either come to me or ride all the way to Hultail, and the smith there is . . . well, no artist with an anvil."

The tea was finished steeping, and he proudly presented me with a cup. I took a sip. It smelled like seaweed but tasted like . . . decomposed seaweed. I smiled and nodded anyway and made myself take another sip.

"You know," Durn said after nearly draining his cup with one long, scalding swallow, "there is one lad who Dovo had a real rivalry with—that Rolf. Rolf the Roofer, Dovo always called him."

"Yes," I said. "The one who's got his cap set for Mayella Meadowbrock."

"That's him. A stout worker, but an ill-tempered sort. Gets in fights nearly every week. His father was in the other day and told me he worries about him. Nearly beat a fellow to death over in Thunderstone. The other fellow started it, but Rolf sure enough finished it."

"Did Dovo ever mention him to you?"

"Oh, yes, told me he enjoyed playing up to Mayella just to drive Rolf wild." Durn cocked his head. "You think maybe he drove Rolf a little *too* wild?"

The thought had certainly occurred to me. "Possible, I suppose. What was Dovo's manner in the smithy like?" I asked. "Did he get along with customers?"

"Yes, most of them. Some he rubbed the wrong way with his joking. When he found someone's weak spot, he'd play on it, you know? Then I'd have to . . . take him in hand a bit." His eyebrows raised as though he had just thought of something. "Just the other day in the smithy he had a run-in with the king's envoy, what's his name?"

"Grodoveth?"

"That's the one. His horse had thrown a shoe, and we were putting one on, when Dovo starts asking the envoy a lot of questions about what he's seen on his journeys, just run of the mill questions, but with an edge to them, almost as though he's making fun of the man.

"Well, I finish the shoeing, and Dovo is leading the horse out while the envoy's paying me, and something happens, the horse stumbles a bit, and this Grodoveth suddenly goes mad. He clouts Dovo on the side of the head, knocking him down, and then stands over him. If he made another move, I was ready to help Dovo, but he didn't. He just said, 'Be careful how you treat my horse, boy,' and that was all.

"He finishes paying me, then without another look at Dovo, leads his horse out. It's a magnificent beast all right, and maybe Dovo did yank its bridle too hard, but that was quite a clout. Still, some men love their horses better than women." Durn eyed my cup. "More tea?"

I declined, thanked him for the information, and left him for the happier cups of the Bold Bard. I hoped I wouldn't have seaweed on my breath. There were a lot of people I wanted to talk to.

14

And they all seemed to be at the tavern that evening. Nothing fills a drinking establishment quite as handily as a tragedy. People want to talk about it, and also want to feel alive and grateful that they were not the one to die. How people can feel more alive in a hot, smoky, reeking tavern than outside in the fresh air on a hilltop gazing up at the evening sky is puzzling, but human nature has always been so.

The first person I noticed in the press of people there was Mayor Tobald. A huge, half-eaten pork pie was on the table in front of him, and he was digging into what was left with his customary ardor for victuals—his way of feeling alive, I suppose.

Since I was acting under his authority, I felt that put us on an equal footing in the democracy of the tavern, so I sat across from him and bade him a good evening. "Ah, Jasper," he responded, "and how goes your work?"

I didn't wish to spill too many beans before I had a

chance to talk to Benelaius. "Not too well, Mayor. But I'll persevere."

"Good man," Tobald said, wrapping his mouth around another forkful.

"Yes, I asked Grodoveth if he was aware of any brigands who might have been responsible for Dovo's slaying, but he knew of no such parties."

"Hmm, yes, well, if anyone would know, you'd think it'd be him. I mean to say, riding around all the time as he does, eh?"

"Indeed, sir. I was just wondering, sir, how did you come to know him?"

"He was my student at the university."

"University?"

"Yes, the University of Suzail. I taught there, you know, before my retirement. The academic life held too many pressures. A small, unhurried town like Ghars was much more appealing to me—just like the feelings of your master Benelaius—and more conducive to my scholarship. I'm writing a history of Cormyr, you know." I knew. Everyone in the village knew.

"When Grodoveth was assigned as envoy to our district," he went on, "I invited him to lodge at my house when he came through Ghars. He accepted, and I learned that he plays as fine a game of chess as any man in the village. That alone would be enough for me to put up with his . . . well, I mean to say, I've enjoyed his company immensely."

There was something that Tobald wasn't saying, but I didn't quite know how to tactfully draw it out. "So he stays with you whenever he's in town?" Tobald chewed and nodded. "And how often is that?"

"Oh, every few weeks or so. It's only for a night or two, and I've got the room, not having a missus. Let that be a lesson to you, Jasper. Marry now. Don't put it off like I did, or you'll wind up a lonely old man like me." He wrinkled up his face as a twinge of pain went through him. "And a gouty old man. Do me a favor, Jasper, and ask your master to mix up another batch of those gout pills he made for me. I didn't want to say anything earlier today in front of Doctor Braum." He sighed. "That man couldn't cure a nosebleed with a wagon load of cotton."

"Certainly, sir."

"And perhaps he could give me an examination sometime. I've not been feeling well, not well at all, and Braum can't find anything wrong except for my gout. You know what he tells me? Eat less. Well, I mean to say, eat less? This is the advice of a trained physician?"

"I'm sure my master will be happy to do what he can, and I'll tell him about the pills."

"Thank you, Jasper. No man could have a better prize than a good and faithful servant."

It wasn't any of Tobald's business, but I was going to be good and faithful for only three more days. Then it was the high road for me, and a life, perhaps, of criminal investigation, depending on how this particular case came out. Now it was time to investigate further. "Have you seen Barthelm Meadowbrock today?"

"Oh, yes," said Tobald. "I was helping him prepare for the arrival of our merchant dignitaries. So little time and so much to do. Barthelm seems nearly exhausted, and we have only two more days until the great event."

"Exhausted, say you?"

The mayor nodded. "Poor man, his eyes are as weary as death. He told me he was up all night worrying when he was not working."

Up all night, I thought. Worrying and working? Or

getting revenge on a man who insulted his daughter? "The incident with his daughter can hardly have helped him sleep any better," I said.

"With Mayella?" I thought Tobald's voice softened somewhat. Our mayor was not yet *that* old, it seemed. "It is true," he said, "young men do seem to make fools of themselves in her presence." And, I could have added, a few older ones as well, remembering Tobald's encounter with Mayella's yapping little dog. "But I suppose that's something that any father of a beautiful daughter must deal with. Even my friend Grodoveth was not immune to her charms. Ah, here he comes now!"

I turned and saw Grodoveth coming in the front door. He looked none too happy to see me talking with Tobald, so I begged my leave of the mayor and retreated to the bar, with Grodoveth's glower following me as I went.

Shortshanks brought me a Golden Sands and I sipped it gratefully. It had been a long day, what with retrieving Lindavar, finding Dovo's body, and making Benelaius's required investigations, and the cold brew tasted wonderful. I ordered a pork pie, since Tobald's had looked so tempting, and wondered if Camber Fosrick felt as weary at the end of a day of sleuthing.

By the time I was finished with my flaky treat, the tavern had fallen into that comfortable state where everyone had started a new glass and no one, not even Sunfirth, was scurrying to take or bring orders. Even Shortshanks looked relaxed, so I tried to engage him in conversation, recalling how Camber Fosrick would gain invaluable clues from barkeeps.

"Heard about Dovo?" I asked him.

He nodded but didn't speak. You really had to touch a chord within Shortshanks to open him up.

The dwarf took pride in his memory, so I decided to try that tack.

"I was trying to remember," I went on, "when the so-called ghost first started appearing. You recall?"

"Mirtul."

At least it was a word. "End of Mirtul? Or the beginning?"

"End."

I had to be careful—the words were getting shorter. "Benelaius and I just couldn't remember who said they saw it . . . and when. I don't suppose you'd remember."

Yes, it was heavy-handed, but it worked. At the suggestion of a slight against his attic of a brain, Shortshanks turned and gave me the evil eye. "Of course I'd remember. Ye think I'd forget a short little list like that? What else was everyone in here talkin' about at those times but this phony ghost and the fools who'd seen it?

" 'Twas at the beginnin' of spring. Dovo was the first, though he lied about it. The twenty-seventh of Mirtul it was. That merchant from Arabel espied it on the twelfth of Kythorn. Mayor Tobald seen it the night after the flower festival—that was the twenty-first of Kythorn. Kythorn the twenty-seventh 'twas Diccon Picard. Then on the eighth of Flamerule Loony Liz spotted it; Flamerule"—he paused for a moment, ticking through the days in his head—"twenty-first it was when Lukas Spoondrift seen it. Then nobody seen it again until Farmer Bortas and his wife on the sixteenth of Eleasias! And the last was Bryn Goldtooth, the halfling, on . . . ah, yes, the twenty-eighth of last month!" Shortshanks cried triumphantly. Then he gave a dwarven smirk. "Comin' back from the Swamp Rat he was. Swore he'd never go on that road after dark again."

I shook my head admiringly. "Your memory, Shortshanks, is as impressive as the brews you serve. I take it that, uh, your trade has increased since the late Dovo's little pranks began?"

"Best thing that could've happened to the Bold Bard," he said. "Got to where folks didn't like travelin' the swamp road after dark, and that was just fine by me." Then he sighed. "A course, now that the ghost's a phony, more folks'll probably be goin' to the Swamp Rat again."

"I wonder," I mused. "There may not be a ghost out there now, but there is a murderer."

He didn't smile, but his mouth didn't curve down as much as usual. "Aye," he said quietly. "Seems there's a bright side after all, then."

15

Though Shortshanks's information was given at lightning speed, still, like all great sleuths, I was able to retain it. How? Simply by writing frantically with a charcoal pencil on a piece of paper under the bar, while watching the dwarf as he spoke.

I feared, however, that I might not be able to decipher my blind scribbling later, so while the names and dates were fresh in my memory, I wanted to polish my scrawl so that I wouldn't wonder later if some number was an eight or a nine.

I walked to the back of the common room and went through a battered door into an enclosed walkway that led to the necessary room of the tavern. In the privacy of the small, unpleasant chamber, a guttering lantern provided enough light to see what I had written. A few characters and numbers were barely legible, but I corrected them and emended the list so that it now read:

Chet Williamson

Mirtul 27-Dovo
Kythorn 12-Arabel merch.
Kythorn 21-Tobald
Kythorn 27-Diccon Picard
Flamerule 8-Liz Clawthorn
Flamerule 21-Lukas Spoondrift
Eleasias 16-Farmer Bortas & wife
Eleasias 28-Bryn Goldtooth
Eleint 16-Jasper

Well, that was a start. Toward what and for what purpose, I wasn't sure, but at least it would show Benelaius I had been on the job.

I tucked the piece of paper in a pocket over my heart, but the pencil slipped out of my hands and rolled under the door to a small closet that I assumed held cleaning materials. I opened the door and saw a bucket on a rope, a broom, and a pile of rags. The pencil had rolled under the rags, so I reached under and felt around for it. I found the pencil, but I found some other things, too.

And what I found first was moving.

It was soft and furry, and when I felt it pour over my hand I leapt back with a yelp, nearly falling onto the necessary seat. But it was only a nest of young mice, old enough to run but too frightened to leave their first home. I sighed in relief and resumed the search for my pencil. And that's when I found what really got my attention.

Beneath the rags was a hat and a cloak, not new but not ready for the rag pile either. The cloak was far too large for me, as was the hat. They were rather nondescript garments save for one thing—there was an ornament on the hat made from a feather and a sigil of the smith's guild, and I had seen Dovo wear it many times.

If this wasn't a clue, I wouldn't have recognized one if it bit me in my buttocks. I rolled up the cloak and hat and put them under my own cloak. It made a lump, but I thought that I could get through the dimly lit Bold Bard easily enough without someone yelling, "Hey, what's that you got under your cloak?"

And so it transpired. I was afraid that Shortshanks would accuse me of leaving without paying, but I slipped out when his back was turned, thanks to my stealthy halfling blood, put the garments in my saddlebag, and came back into the inn, where I ordered a second drink.

I thought about what else I might do to gather more evidence, and it seemed it would be a good idea to try and determine who on my list of suspects was right-handed, and who was left, since it had been concluded that the killer struck with his right hand. First I observed the tables.

There was Grodoveth, who was looking fishier and fishier as the day had worn on. But he clasped his mug with his left hand, and put it down only to dig into a large venison steak with a fork, frequently bumping the constantly moving right hand of Tobald across the table. Grodoveth was a left-hander then, but I still didn't trust him.

As luck would have it, Barthelm came in several minutes later. He nodded at Tobald and coldly ignored Grodoveth. Nor did he acknowledge Rolf, who had come in when I was in the necessary. The old merchant went up to the service area at the end of the bar nearest the door and bade Shortshanks to infuse him a small pot of coffee, that black beverage brewed from crushed, charred beans from far Durpar. I've heard it refreshes the mind, but it's too rich for my poor purse.

As I watched Barthelm from the corner of my eye,

I saw that everything he did, from paying the dwarf to pouring cream into his cup and lifting it, he did with his right hand. Barthelm drank two cups of the evil-smelling brew and left. Back to work, no doubt, getting ready for the bigwigs.

I watched Rolf then, and he seemed to be his old cantankerous self. Sour faced, he sat with both big hands wrapped around his mug, favoring neither one hand nor the other but drinking with both.

Then I remembered a trick Camber Fosrick had played in *The Adventure of the Battledale Billhook* to discover which hand a suspect favored. He had suddenly thrown a ball at the man, who had caught it with his left hand (a hand that, supposedly, he could not even use), proving him to be a killer. So I ordered from Shortshanks a small round nut cheese and waited until Rolf's attention was distracted.

He was sitting at the short end of the bar, several stools away from me. I called out, "Rolf!" and tossed the cheese toward him. His drinking must have slowed his reaction time, for although he looked up, he made no attempt to catch the cheese, which hit him squarely in the forehead and then fell into his mug, splashing him with ale.

Dead silence fell upon the Bold Bard, as all eyes went to the ale-sodden Rolf, who looked first at the cheese in his mug and then at me with a basilisk glare. The look demanded, if not my blood, at least an explanation.

"I, uh . . . I thought you might like some cheese," I said.

That apparently was not the explanation he was looking for. He stood up, came over to me, and showed me in no uncertain terms that he was indeed right-handed.

After I picked myself up off the floor, rubbing my

aching jaw and checking with my tongue to see how many of my teeth had been loosened, he took another swipe at me, but the blow only grazed me, for Shortshanks had vaulted over the bar with his mallet in hand. The dwarf grabbed the back of Rolf's trousers and lifted, throwing Rolf off balance and propelling him straight ahead toward the front door. Rolf's head smashed the door open, and the roofer's body followed it through, given extra impetus by the flat of the mallet laid to his posterior.

"Come back when ye're in not sich a dark mood!" Shortshanks cried. "This is a happy tavern!" Then without a smile he pulled shut the door and glared at me. "And you—don't be so free with your cheese!"

The dwarf reacted not at all to the howls of laughter from his clientele. He simply went behind the bar and stowed his mallet, and I continued to massage my sore jaw. Rolf, I thought, was a person who would kill a body just as soon as look at him. I wondered what Mayella saw in him. But sometimes women are like that, showing a fondness for the most bestial types. It would not have been beyond such a wretch to have lopped off Dovo's head for the sheer joy of it.

I toyed with the idea of following him, but I liked not the thought of what he might do if he caught me spying on him. No, I decided, that might best be left for another day.

My nearly full Golden Sands had been spilled in the scuffle, so I ordered another, and decided I would return home to Benelaius after it was emptied.

Grodoveth and Tobald were finally finished eating, and I noticed that Grodoveth signed the bill, which Sunfirth entered into the account book kept behind the bar. From Grodoveth's appearance at the Bold Bard the night before, and from his sense of comfort and the fact that he had his own account there, I assumed he frequented the place often. And that account book, I realized, would tell me precisely when Grodoveth had been in Ghars.

There was no way, I well knew, to leisurely examine the book there in the tavern. But if I could get it out of thetavern . . .

The book was small enough to easily hide beneath my cloak, if I was able to get it in the first place. A distraction would be ideal, but I dismissed the idea of tossing another cheese. The tosser and the tossee fall under equal scrutiny, and I wanted the attention drawn away from me and my end of the bar.

So I pondered while I paid my bill and finished my brew. Then I remembered some little friends of mine.

Two trips to the necessary room in one evening of drinking excites no curiosity, and when I returned to the common room my capacious sleeves were not quite as roomy. I waited until Sunfirth was behind the bar, and then, when no one was looking, I allowed six small mice to run out of my sleeves onto the bar top, and another half dozen to take their chances on the floor.

The effect was more than I had hoped for. Sunfirth gave a cunning little scream and began slapping at the mice with her bar rag, shouting a wordless "Ah! Ah! Ah!" with every blow.

"Vermin!" yelled Shortshanks, who was in front of the bar. "Vermin in my tavern!" He dove behind the bar, nearly knocking over Sunfirth, grabbed his mallet, and proceeded to play whack-a-mouse on the tavern floor while Sunfirth played slap-a-rat on the bar, and the patrons cheered.

In the midst of this merriment, no one noticed yours truly, the founder of the fun, slip behind the bar, slide the account book into my once again empty sleeve, and sidle off into the night. The account book joined Dovo's cloak and hat in my saddlebag, and I untied Jenkus, mounted him, and rode south out of town.

16

I had scarcely gone fifty yards when I heard the sound behind me of people coming out of the Bold Bard. At first I thought my theft had been discovered, and that a posse of barflies was coming in hot pursuit. But then I saw that they were only patrons who had had enough excitement for one night and were seeking another watering hole, heading for the more respectable bars of the two inns in town, or the scruffier environs of the Swamp Rat.

Among the escapees were the unmistakable figures of round Mayor Tobald and massive Grodoveth, who mounted their steeds and, instead of heading toward the mayor's dwelling just north of town, rode south in my direction. That meant, I surmised, that they were heading to the Swamp Rat, and I spurred Jenkus on, thinking to stay well ahead of them and be at the swampside tavern long before they arrived. There were many things that I didn't like about Grodoveth, and I wanted to observe him further, particularly near the spot where Dovo's murder had taken place.

I arrived at the Swamp Rat without incident. A couple of anxious drinkers had galloped past me on the way, but I met no one headed toward Ghars. As I have said, the Swamp Rat was a less than elegant establishment. Sawdust and crushed oyster shells littered the floor, as did one or two heavy imbibers. The lights were as low as a goblin's belly, and jars of greenish pickled eggs sat on the bar, looking about as appetizing as ogre eyeballs.

But they did serve ale, cheap ale at a cheap price, and that was the Swamp Rat's chief attraction, along with its location, as far as the local farmhands were concerned. I ordered a light ale, which Hesketh Pratt, the owner and sole worker, presented with less than a flourish, but with a smarmy smile on his ratlike face. He was the perfect man to own a tavern called the Swamp Rat. With the first sip of my ale, I knew that its lightness was due to added water. Shortshanks had been right on that count.

After I had removed a small bug from the surface of my glass and taken a few more sips, Grodoveth and Tobald entered. Tobald smiled and hailed me. "Ah, young Jasper! Had enough of the old rat race in town, have you? Rat race? Eh?"

I smiled and nodded. "One more before home and sleep, Mayor. I pray little fuzzy things don't haunt my dreams."

Tobald chuckled and sat nearby with Grodoveth, who had been watching me with an emotionless face. I in turn sat and watched Grodoveth, by way of a smoky mirror over the bar. There was little else to do. The Swamp Rat's patrons were sturdy farmer types whose conversation this night mostly consisted of:

"Hear about that, what's 'is name, that feller whut died."

"Devo, was it?"

"Nah, 'twasn't that . . . ah, Dovo."

"Aye. Quite a thing."

"Aye. Murdered he was."

"Aye. Quite a thing."

"Don't know what this world's comin' to."

"Aye. Don't know."

"So how's the barley?"

It could go on like that for hours. At least I had one stroke of luck, if you can call it that. I learned that Farmer Bortas, one of those who Shortshanks told me had seen Dovo's fake ghost, was sitting in the corner with two other rude tillers of the soil. I went over and introduced myself as Benelaius's servant. His crinkly old eyes lit up.

"Benelaius's lad, are ye? Sure and it's good to have a wizard in our midst, a fine gentleman like that, though I never met 'im mysel'. You met 'im, Rob? Will?"

Rob and Will clutched their pipes firmly in their jaws and shook their heads. "Don't cotton to wizards mysel'," Will stated out of a corner of his mouth. "Seems unnatural, like."

"Aye," agreed Rob.

I figured the only way to get into all of their good graces was to buy them drinks, so I made the offer and they accepted, ordering a pitcher of Shadowdark ale, the most pricey beverage the Swamp Rat served.

"Thankee, young man," Farmer Bortas said heartily, but the two others merely nodded their thanks, apparently not "cottonin' " to wizards' servants either.

"So I understand," I said, getting to it, "that you saw this phony ghost that this fellow who got killed was playing?"

A cloud gathered on Bortas's face. "Aye, I saw it all right—or I saw *him*, the cheap faker! Scared me and my good wife out of a week's sleep, it did. She still wakes up screamin', 'O, 'tis the ghost, 'tis the ghost!' and I has to tell her no, it ain't the ghost, he's back in the swamp. Now I guess I'll be tellin' her there weren't no ghost to begin with."

"What was he—this Dovo chap—doing when you saw him?" I asked.

"Hauntin'. My wife seen 'im first. She grabs me by the arm and says real sharp, 'Look!' and I look and there he is. 'Twas about a quarter mile west of here, where the road curves down closest to the swamp. His face is all green and glowin' and he starts moanin' and walks toward us slow like, swingin' his axe back and forth. Fair gave me the willies, it did. How's I to know it wasn't real? So's I put the whip to old Ned and we tuck off down the road and didn't slow down till we gets here. We runs inside and tells 'em all what I seen, and a whole bunch of us goes back to where I seen it—Rob 'n Will, you was both there, wasn't you?"

"Aye," said Rob and Will in unison.

"But there weren't nothin' there. Not a blessed thing. Like that man just sunk into the very earth."

"You searched around then?"

"Oh aye, we searched—just to the edge of the swamp, mind. It took enough gumption just fer us to go that near the swamp at night. But we found nary a thing."

"Was he carrying anything other than the axe?" I asked, remembering the pieces of broken lantern glass.

"He could've had an oliphant in his other hand for all I knew. I just saw that axe a-swingin', and that was enough for me and the missus."

"But nothing else . . . glowing?"

"Just his face. Like a corpse it was." He shook his head with a mixture of disgust and regret. "And like a corpse he is now, sure enough. Met up with someone who played a trick right back on 'im, rest his soul." Then he beamed at me again. "But lookin' at the bright side, we got no ghost spookin' around anymore." A similar sentiment, I thought, to Shortshanks's.

The conversation changed to farming then, but I noticed that Grodoveth and Tobald were standing up, Tobald brushing crumbs off his shirtfront. I strained to hear what they were saying over Farmer Bortas's droning about oats, and caught Grodoveth saying, ". . . too tired to ride back. I'll just spend the night here."

And Tobald replied, "Well, I've got to get up early and help Barthelm. Are you sure? I hate riding back alone. . . ."

Then Bortas said something, but I just managed to catch Grodoveth's words: ". . . no more ghost. What's there to be scared of?" He turned to Hesketh Pratt. "I'll be staying here tonight."

Hesketh bowed deeply and licked his lips, I supposed, at the thought of a paying lodger. "Very good, Lord Grodoveth. I'll show you upstairs. . . ."

"I'll find it," said Grodoveth, and clapped a hand on Tobald's shoulder. "Sleep well, my friend. I know I shall." And so saying, he went upstairs with a candle that Hesketh handed him. Tobald paid Hesketh for the drinks and, giving me a farewell wave, went outside.

I excused myself from the somnolent discussion, left enough on the table to pay for the drinks, fearing that Benelaius would be annoyed by my profligacy, and went to the door. Hearing hoofbeats, I peered out and saw that Tobald was indeed heading west toward the road to Ghars, looking uneasily about him.

There was no one else outside, so I stepped across the road and looked up at the six second-floor windows. A candle gleamed through the thin curtain that covered one of them, and the shadow's flickering told me that someone was moving inside. After a few minutes the light went out, leaving the window in utter darkness. I waited another minute, and then walked around to the back of the tavern.

There was only one door that led to the outside from the kitchen, and two windows. Only one small second-story window looked out on the swamp, so I figured the upstairs back consisted of a poorly lit hall.

I remained for another half hour, going from front to back, but Grodoveth's room remained dark, and no one came out of the tavern save for Farmer Bortas and his friends. I stayed in the shadows so they didn't see me.

After their departure, Jenkus and I started for home. It was perhaps a mile from the Swamp Rat to Benelaius's cottage, and I confess I started to drowse almost the instant I was in the saddle. Jenkus's walking gait is very soothing to the weary soul, and I was nothing if not weary.

I suppose I dreamed the footsteps before I actually heard them. But when they came into my waking mind, I knew that I had not heard the like before. It sounded like two or three horses running behind me with loose shoes, a jittery, clattery kind of sound. But after each clatter was a great thud, so that I knew there was great weight falling on the road. It was a constant *da-da-BOOM, da-da-BOOM* behind me, and from the sound of it, it was getting closer and closer.

Chet Williamson

Jenkus had significantly increased his speed on his own, but I spurred him nonetheless before I looked around. When I *did* look around, I spurred him harder

17

It was pitch-black, and we were keeping to the road more by instinct than sight, but I was able to see against the sky behind me what looked like a small mass of men and horses riding all together. Men and horses? Say rather ogres on oliphants. I swung my head around and didn't dare to look back again.

But I did call back to them, "What is it you want?" thinking that if they cried out, "Your purse!" or "Your life!" they would be less frightening. But there was only silence except for the *da-da-BOOM*, which now sounded to me like a drum beating my death knell.

Now I dug my heels into Jenkus's flanks, and he responded wonderfully. I think he was even more frightened than I. He whinnied frantically and put on a burst of speed that ruffled my cloak and blew my hair straight back. I clung to the reins with one hand and the saddlebag with the other, not wanting to lose my ill-gotten evidence.

If we outdistanced the party behind, we would be

safe at Benelaius's house, thanks to that spell of protection, one of the few spells he had cast since his retirement. It would keep out anything evil unless it were specifically invited, and I certainly didn't intend to invite whatever was behind me.

Whatever it was, it was falling behind, giving me the leisure to think about what it could be. A band of brigands, the same ones who might have killed Dovo the night before? No, there weren't enough footprints for a band. Then maybe a posse mistaking me for the killer? Hardly—I'd surely have known about any posse that had formed.

Or was it even, I thought with a chill that shivered me from neck to seat, the ghost of Fastred, tired of such foolishness in his name, galumphing along on hands and feet of razor-sharp axe blades?

Well, whatever it had been, it was gone now. I heard those thunderous, ratcheting footfalls no more. Jenkus and I were making thunderous footfalls of our own. I tried to pull him back to a trot as we neared the safety of the cottage, but he would have none of it, continuing to gallop until I pulled him up hard right by the stable door.

"Well done, Jenkus!" I said as I dismounted. "I didn't know you had it in you!"

Neither did Jenkus, apparently, for he was quite exhausted, just like his rider. Before I was even done unsaddling him, Benelaius and Lindavar came rushing out of the house toward me. Well, Lindavar was rushing, lantern held high. I couldn't see my master's feet, so he seemed to follow in Lindavar's wake like a large leather ball bobbing after a swimmer.

"We heard you galloping in," said Lindavar breathlessly. "Is aught amiss?"

"No, everything's fine—now."

"My boy," said Benelaius, "such haste is unseemly.

It alarms young men"—he nodded at Lindavar—"and makes old ones come out in the night damps."

"Well, you see, master, something was—"

"Pursuing you," Benelaius interrupted. "Yes, that much seemed clear." Then he looked about at the night. "I take it, however, that the pursuer was unable to breach the protective spell."

"Frankly," I said, "I don't think it even got this far." I patted Jenkus affectionately, but he only snorted in annoyance. "Jenkus outran it."

"Imagine that," said the old mage. "I didn't think dear Jenkus was capable of outrunning anything, except perhaps a sailor with two wooden legs. Rheumatic ones at that." He turned and started to walk back toward the house. "Get your equine savior rubbed down, Jasper. Then come in for something warm, and you can report to us what you've learned from your day in town"—he turned back—"and at the Swamp Rat, I see."

"Wha . . . but how did you . . . ?"

He gave no answer but went inside, arm in arm with Lindavar.

After getting Jenkus fed and settled in for the night, I went inside. Benelaius and Lindavar were sitting with large earthen mugs of raspberry tea, among the cats in front of the fire. I filled my own mug, gently jostled a few felines aside, and joined them.

"So tell us," said Benelaius, stroking a tabby, "precisely everything you did, heard, and saw. In detail."

And I did, almost exactly as I have set it down here. Its telling took longer to Benelaius, for he interrupted frequently to ask questions, most of which, though I answered, I could not see as being of any import.

It was after two o'clock by the time the tale was

told, concluding with my narrow escape on the
swamp road. Benelaius nodded, glanced again at
the account book and garments I had brought back,
and at the list I had made in the Bold Bard. "It is
late," he said, "and we should not attempt any
deductions with dull minds. I suggest we retire and
discuss the meanings of all this in the morning."

Even though greatly fatigued, I was still disappointed not to hear what Benelaius thought of my
work, and what conclusions he might draw. He
sensed my dismay, and patted me on the shoulder.
"Well done, Jasper. You've learned much. And on
the morrow, we shall hopefully make much of it."

"May I ask but one question, master?" I said from
the top of the stairs.

"Go ahead."

"How were you so certain that I was at the Swamp
Rat?"

"Your clothing," said he, "bears the odor of West
Fennet Number Three, a pipeweed that the tobac-
conist in town refuses to carry because of its bitter
aftertaste. Farmer Snaggard, having gathered a
fondness for it in youth, grows a small plot of it
every year for his own use only, and he has been an
inveterate patron of the Swamp Rat since it opened.
I assumed that, since you had not been likely to visit
Farmer Snaggard, who lives far down the west
swamp road, that you must have shared the closed
air of the Swamp Rat with him."

Both Lindavar and I gaped open mouthed at him.
"That's . . . that's an incredible deduction!" I said.

Benelaius beamed at the compliment, then
seemed to think of something else. "Oh, and, of
course," he said, "you have a bit of something stuck
to your shoe. Green is such an unseemly shade for
pickled eggs, isn't it?"

18

I fell asleep upon the instant but had bad dreams all
night long. They began with a nightmare about
Dovo's corpse. I was alone and waiting for Lindavar
to return with Benelaius, when Dovo's head started
rolling back toward his body. As I watched in horror,
it reattached itself to the sodden stump, and the
armor-clad body pushed itself to its feet.

But the head was on backward, and the corpse
crouched, moving like a blind man, its face toward
the sky, feeling its way across the mushy turf until its
gray fingers came in contact with—

The axe.

Dovo's corpse picked up the weapon and straightened up, and the gaze of the dead eyes fell on me. I
could not move. Terror rooted me to the spot. The
monstrous thing advanced upon me, but backward. It
shuffled nearer, the dead mouth splitting in Dovo's
idiotic grin, the axe upraised in the right hand. But
since its body was facing away from me, it could not

swing the axe down on me, and instead drew it in front of its body and swung backhand, whirling around—

And I awoke with a gasp, trembling in the darkness.

I lit a candle and lay in bed watching its flame dance for a long time before I trusted myself to go back to sleep.

O foolish trust.

The next dream was worse. In it I was riding at night on the swamp road, but there was a full moon so that I was able to see. Jenkus was trotting along, and behind me I heard again the *da-da-BOOM* I had heard coming home. I spurred Jenkus on, but although he tried to run, it was as if his legs were mired in quicksand. The sound of pounding hooves behind me grew nearer, and I turned my head to look.

There were four huge black horses, their shoulders twice as high as any man's head, their eyes blazing and their snouts puffing smoke and flame. They were riding so closely together that I could scarcely distinguish one from the other.

But if they were frightening, their riders were worse. They were people I knew, people who were among the suspects in Dovo's death, but these were full-fledged nightmare versions.

Kendra's red hair had become crimson snakes, and her mouth gaped wide, showing fangs. Rolf was a huge, brutal man-ape, like some troglodytic force of malevolence. Next to him was Barthelm, whose full features had grown into rolls of yellowish fat flesh that poured down over his steed. And finally there was Grodoveth, looking like some legendary warrior-king, helmeted and cuirassed, with both weapon-wielding hands raised above his head. In one hand was a sword, in the other an axe. There were axes in the hands of all of them, and they were closing quickly, looming over me.

I urged Jenkus on, but to no avail. As I watched, the four riders merged until they were but one creature, a behemoth with many heads and many blades, all of them intent on taking my life. Now my breathing seemed as slow as Jenkus's pace. Frantically I struggled to get more air into my lungs, thinking that if I did, then I could scream, and if I screamed, then I would wake up and these horrors would vanish.

But I could not breathe, and I turned away from my pursuers, back toward Jenkus, and he turned his head toward me.

And I looked into the dead, staring eyes of Dovo.

Apparently that was the shock I needed. I awoke with my face buried in my pillow, trying to suck the feathers through the cotton. I pushed the pillow away and gasped, grateful to the gods for the joy of awakening from nightmare.

It was light outside, and the shaft of sunlight on my wall told me it was about seven-thirty. I considered getting up and preparing breakfast for my master and his guest, but everyone had been up so late the night before that I felt another hour of rest wouldn't hurt. Going back to sleep in the daylight, I hoped, would bring no more nightmares.

But just before I dozed back off, I heard the front door of the cottage close, and opened an eye. I knew Benelaius's spell was good against any intruder, so I assumed it was my master coming back from a morning constitutional. He went out occasionally to study the flora and fauna immediately surrounding the cottage. Still, I listened for a moment, and heard only Lindavar's rhythmic snores from the guest room next to my own.

When I next had a waking thought, it was about how Grimalkin was able to have such soft fur and such a rough tongue. I opened my eyes at nine o'clock to find Grimalkin standing on my chest, pressing his soft nose against my cheeks to wake me, and giving my chin a quick lick with his tongue. One needs no water clock with Benelaius's brilliant menagerie.

I arose, washed, and went downstairs. First I fed the cats, and then went to the stable to take care of the horses. Both Jenkus and Stubbins were slow to rally. I could understand Jenkus's sloth. He had galloped hard the night before, and perhaps he too may have been having bad dreams about our pursuer. He had seemed just as scared as I was at the time.

But I didn't know what was keeping Stubbins from leaping to his oats. I had to call him three times before he finally joined Jenkus at breakfast.

"Now where'd you get that?" I asked him, noticing a spot of mud on his fetlock. I must have neglected to rub it off after our carriage journey yesterday. Stubbins chewed while I rubbed, and after cleaning his leg I went back inside to see to human breakfast.

I heard Lindavar and Benelaius moving about upstairs while I brewed a large pot of tea and prepared a sumptuous feast of eggs, smoked salmon, elven bread, and the special sausages that Benelaius adores. By the time they came down, fully dressed, I had everything on the table, piping hot and ready to eat.

"Ah, Jasper," said Benelaius, "you truly are a wonder. Investigating all day and half the night, troubled by nightmares the other half, and still you greet us with a magnificent breakfast."

"Um . . . how did you know I had nightmares?"

"When I hear heavy breathing followed by tiny

cries in the middle of the night—and I know that you sleep alone—that is the only conclusion. Come, Lindavar, Jasper, sit. Let us fill our bellies with this most excellent breakfast, and then, over tea, discuss the events of this past day."

We ate heartily, and then, as we were emptying the teapot, Benelaius started asking questions. "So, Jasper, from all your observations, who do you suspect of having killed Dovo?"

"I think there are several possibilities," I said, pleased that my opinion as well as my findings were requested. "Dovo angered a number of people in the tavern the night he was killed. Rolf and Dovo fought over Dovo's advances to Mayella."

"Is Rolf capable of murder, do you think?"

"He could be, master. His temper is short, he seems quite violent, and if he came upon Dovo playing his ghost trick . . ." I shrugged.

"True," Lindavar said. "His anger at being gulled combined with jealousy—it makes for an uneasy combination in one so ill-tempered."

"Who else?" asked Benelaius.

"Barthelm, possibly. A father will go to great lengths to defend his daughter's honor."

"In which case," my master added with a crooked smile, "Grodoveth had best look out, eh?"

I nodded. "Kendra would be another suspect. Dovo was quite offensive to her, and if she were to come upon Fastred's ghost, she is not the type who would run. She might very well strike before she knew the ghost was a hoax. And she cannot account for her whereabouts."

"And what about Grodoveth?" asked Lindavar. "From what Aunsible Durn told you, Jasper, he was furious at Dovo for some reason."

Benelaius gently removed the cats from his lap,

stood up, waddled over to the sideboard, and took from it the cloak and hat that had belonged to Dovo. "And what do these suggest?"

I looked at Lindavar, wondering if it wasn't his turn again, but he didn't want the ball. "They suggest," I said, "that Dovo might have been using the Bold Bard as a center of operations, hiding his clothes there while he engaged in his ghostly masquerade."

"Have we discussed," Benelaius said, "the matter of who stood to benefit most from the appearance of the ghost?"

"I would think," Lindavar said, "that it would be this dwarf who owns the Bold Bard . . . what was it, Shortlegs?"

"Shortshanks," I corrected. "That's true. Anything that kept folks away from the Swamp Rat would help the Bold Bard." I grinned. "Maybe Shortshanks supplies them with their watered ale and pickled eggs."

" 'There's more to me than you might think,' " Benelaius quoted. "Dovo said that to Kendra, correct?"

"Yes . . ." I thought for a moment. "You think that Dovo might have been playing ghost to—"

"To help Shortshanks!" Lindavar said. "That makes sense. But was Shortshanks in on it?"

"I doubt if Dovo has ever done a thing in his life," I said, "except for profit or to impress a woman. I think it altogether possible that the dwarf hired Dovo to scare people away from the Swamp Rat."

"You know, there's another possibility that's just occurred to me," Lindavar said. "Jasper, you said just now that Kendra might have struck before she even knew the ghost was a counterfeit. What then would prevent some other armed and fearless traveler from doing the same?"

"A random occurrence, you mean," said Benelaius.

"A reasonable hypothesis. But we may be overlooking something." From beneath Dovo's cloak, he took out the account book from the Bold Bard. "Have you had a chance to look at this, Jasper?" I shook my head. "Then I suggest you do so now—both of you—along with Jasper's list of ghostly sightings."

He set them on the table, and Lindavar and I pulled our chairs close together to examine the documents. After many minutes of perusal, Lindavar spoke tentatively. "Master Shortshanks appears to keep his books meticulously. Yet I see nothing in the nature of payments made to another party for say, advertisement or promotion. Only money in, money out, this girl Sunfirth's salary, and customers' accounts."

Benelaius eyed me. "Jasper?"

"I think," I said carefully, not wanting to contradict my master's guest, "that Shortshanks might not readily put down on paper evidence of something that is, if not illegal, then at least of doubtful, um . . . scrupulosity."

"I think the word you're searching for is *scrupulousness*," said Benelaius, "though *integrity* may be more correct. But you make a good point. Shortshanks would doubtless make any such payments off the books. And speaking of books, what else do you find there? In conjunction with your list, Jasper?"

We compared the dates with the account book entries. The answer was obvious, and I let Lindavar make the discovery. "At the time of every ghost sighting but one," he said, "it seems that Grodoveth was passing through the town."

"Yes," I agreed. "From these accounts, it seems that Grodoveth comes to Ghars every two weeks or so, and that also seems to be the interval between most of the sightings. With, as you say, my lord, one"—I looked again—"nay, two exceptions."

"And those are?" asked Benelaius.

"An unnamed Arabel merchant saw the ghost on the twelfth of Kythorn, and Diccon Picard on the twenty-seventh. But Tobald saw the ghost on the twenty-first, when Grodoveth was not in town."

"Or at least not on Shortshanks's books," Lindavar pointed out. "It's possible he was here and didn't go to the tavern."

"I'll check on that," I said.

"Knowing Tobald," said Benelaius, "it's also possible that he saw a wisp of swamp gas or a will-o'-the-wisp and thought he saw a ghost."

That was true. Our mayor, for all his good points, could easily get excited over nothing. "There's a big gap," I said, "between the twenty-first of Flamerule, when Lukas Spoondrift saw Dovo, to the sixteenth of Eleasias, when Bortas and his wife spotted him. And according to the book, Grodoveth was in Ghars on the second and third of Eleasias. So why no ghost then?"

"Maybe he was there," Lindavar suggested, "but no one rode by. It's possible. Or perhaps Dovo didn't go haunting then."

I shook my head in frustration. "I don't understand," I said. "Grodoveth was investigating the legends of the ghost, yes, but what connection could he have to Dovo? How does the appearance of the ghost do him any good?"

Benelaius stroked the tabby perched on his left shoulder. "Let's not get ahead of ourselves. But stop and ask, what do we know about the murderer?"

"That he was right-handed," Lindavar said.

I nodded. "And Grodoveth is left-handed, while everyone else, as far as I know, favors the right hand."

114

"So should we rule Grodoveth out?" asked Lindavar.

"But," said Benelaius, "is your primary conclusion correct?"

"That Grodoveth is left-handed?" I said. "He does everything with his left hand."

"No no. Your *primary* conclusion."

"Ah!" said Lindavar. "You mean the deduction that the killer is right-handed."

Benelaius nodded sagely.

"Well," Lindavar said, "Dovo was certainly facing his killer, and the axe blade struck him on the left side of his neck. . . ."

Then I remembered my dream, and how the reassembled Dovo had swung the axe at me.

"Backhand," I said quietly. "A warrior would swing his axe backhand."

"That is a more powerful stroke," Benelaius said.

"In that case," Lindavar said, "the killer would have used his left hand. Making him left-handed instead of right."

"Quite possibly. And Grodoveth *is* a trained warrior."

"Master," I said. "Are you suggesting that Grodoveth is the killer?"

"I am suggesting nothing. I merely wish for us to get all the facts straight."

"Grodoveth was angry at Dovo at the smithy," Lindavar said, "but making his horse stumble would be no reason for killing him."

"Unless," I added, "he was mad at Dovo about something else, and the horse was just an excuse. Aunsible Durn said that Dovo was asking Grodoveth irritating questions. Maybe the envoy resented them."

Just then the cats began to rise and move *en masse*

toward the front door. In a few seconds we heard the sound of horses' hooves. I opened the door as soon as the knock sounded.

On the small porch stood three men. Mayor Tobald was pale and trembling, and Captain Flim looked his usual stolid self. A third man, whom I didn't know, was with them. He was small and haggard, and his lined and leathery brown skin proclaimed him a gnome.

"Jasper, I must see Benelaius," Tobald said in a rush. "Is he in?"

"Of course, sir. Please, come in."

"Oh, not me, sor," said the gnome in a gravelly voice. "I've got peat and muck all over me boots, I do. Wouldn't want to soil yer foin rugs now, indeed I wouldn't, sor."

"Oh, for mercy sake, Darvik!" said Tobald, who seemed a hairsbreadth from panic. "Come in, man, come in. A little muck won't matter." Easy for him to say, who doesn't have to do the cleaning up of aforesaid muck.

The gnome hesitated, the mayor clucked, and Captain Flim looked impatient with both of them. Benelaius ended the standoff by appearing behind me with Lindavar. "Lord Mayor," he greeted Tobald. "To what do we owe the—"

"The honor of the visit, yes, yes," interrupted Tobald. "Murder, Benelaius! There's been another murder!"

"Oh my my my," said my master. "And who was the victim this time?"

"None other," said Mayor Tobald, "than King Azoun's envoy. Grodoveth is dead!"

19

"Grodoveth?" I said. Speak of the devil.

"Yes, Grodoveth!" said Tobald. His usually ruddy cheeks were pale as ashes. "Murdered!"

"I'm so sorry, Tobald," Benelaius said. "I know he was a friend of yours. But come in, come in and tell me more about this dreadful news."

"But me shoes, sor . . ." said the gnome.

"Oh, that's quite all right, um . . ."

"Darvik's me name, sor," said the solemn little man.

"Well, how do you do, Darvik. I am Benelaius, this is Lindavar, and Jasper is the name of my servant, who will be happy to clean up any soil should you unintentionally deposit some on the interiors. Please, enter."

It would have been rude to refuse my master's gracious invitation, though I wished everyone were not so cavalier about my ability to obliterate swamp muck from carpeting. I winced at every messy step the gnome took. In spite of his muddy state, the cats thronged happily around him, though they remained aloof to both Tobald and Flim.

In the main room, Darvik seated himself on a wooden chair, for which I was thankful since it would clean more easily than upholstery, and at least two dozen cats settled in at his moist feet.

"Now," Benelaius said, "what happened?"

"I left Grodoveth last night at the Swamp Rat," Tobald began. "He was staying the night there because he was too tired to return to Ghars with me. He said he planned to ride south on his duties this morning, and going to Ghars would have meant backtracking as well, so we said farewell. The next thing I know, Captain Flim is knocking on my door to tell me that Grodoveth's dead—*murdered*."

"And where did this occur?" said my master.

"In the swamp," Captain Flim said. "This gnome found him."

With a comforting smile, Benelaius turned to the little creature. "Would you be so kind, Darvik, as to tell me about it?"

"Certainly, sor. I was out pickin' peat, y'see. I pick peat about once a month or so, since Missus Darvik and I use it in the stove, y'know. Burns a heap better than wood, it does, and almos' as good as coal even. Well, sor, there's this one spot that's got grand peat, foin and thick it is, and I've been there afore plenty o' times. You got to know how to get there, though. You don't know how to get there, you'll end up bein' sucked down fer sure, sor. But if you know where to walk, there's solid footin' the whole way. Well, sure there is, isn't there? Or I'd be at the bottom of the swamp now, wouldn't I?"

"Just get *on* with it, man!" said Tobald.

"Right, sor. Well, it takes a heap o' pokin' about

with yer feet to find yer way there, but I done it, and there's a little rocky island there, sor, like a firm rock right in the midst of the swamp, covered with moss. Often had me lunch there, sor, when I'd be pickin' peat, and never thought a thing about it, just that it was nice it was there to have me lunch on. . . ."

"Darvik, *please*," said the mayor.

"Right, sor. Sorry, sor. But anyways, I never seen it with its lid off before."

"Its lid?" Lindavar said.

"Aye, sor. Like a big door it was, right in the middle of the rock where the moss had hid it. A door, only it opened up instead of out."

"A trapdoor, you mean," said Benelaius.

Darvik looked at him as though he had said something worthy of genius. "A trapdoor! That's the very thing, sor. A trapdoor it was. Well, I'd never seen a trapdoor in the middle of the swamp before, so I looked down in and there was steps, sor, leadin' down. I had a candle with me—always carry a candle and flint and steel along, I do, because you never know, no, you don't. So I got a little tinder goin' and lit the candle and went on down, though I don't mind tellin' you, sor, I was a trifle scared, I was. I've seen my share of funny things in that swamp, all right, even in daylight, but the peat's so good there, sor, that I just—"

"Will you please forget the peat and get to the paint . . . er, point," Tobald said.

"Beggin' yer pardon, sor. Well, I went down the stairs, sor, watchin' fer traps an' such, and halfway down I see this light, sor, and I get to the bottom and see it's a torch, only it's fell down from the one who was carryin' it and it's still burnin' on the floor. And then I see the one what was carryin' it, and he looks mighty dead, sor."

"How could you tell he was dead?" Lindavar asked.

"Well, sor, with his head over here and the rest of him over there, it didn't look promisin' for him."

He spoke this last with the same utter earnestness that had graced the rest of his narrative, and I withheld what I feared would sound like a crazy laugh, though I thought I saw Benelaius's lips turn upward just a bit.

"No, sor, he was deader than a fish. A dead fish, I mean to say."

"When you saw the body," Benelaius said, "what did you do?"

"I hightailed out of there, sor. I figgered that whatever done fer him might try and do fer me, and I like me head right where it is, sor."

Benelaius nodded understandingly. "A wise move, under the quite frightening circumstances."

Darvik looked puzzled, then went on. "If you say so, sor. Anyways I ran, and runnin' ain't too smart when you got to think about where to put your feet, and that's how come I got so mucky. But I made it out all right, and run up to the road, and thank the gods, down it is comin' some of the Purple Dragons."

"I was reconnoitering with some of my men," said Captain Flim. "It was lucky we were riding by when this one came up on the road. He took us back to see, and after I saw who it was, I left the men there and rode into town for the mayor. Right away he said he had to see you."

"Benelaius, you must do something," Tobald said. "I mean, Dovo's murder was bad enough, but to have an envoy of King Azoun slaughtered . . . and the king's relative, on top of it!"

"There there, Tobald," said my master. "I know it must come as a terrible shock to you, but I assure you, we shall do everything we can. Have you sent word to Suzail yet?"

Tobald nodded. "Of course. Captain Flim's speediest messenger is on his way even now with the news." He shook his head disconsolately. "Oh, terrible, terrible day," he wailed. "Everything had been going so smoothly for the arrival of the guild council . . . and when my gout kicked up again, I knew something bad was going to happen. But this . . ."

"Ah, yes, your gout," said Benelaius as though he had forgotten. "Jasper did say you needed some more medication, and that you had requested a physical examination as well. I'll tell you what, Tobald, why don't we let Jasper, Lindavar, and Captain Flim go back to the swamp, and you remain here with me. You seem quite distressed, and it would be wise for me to give you a thorough examination now to make sure that nothing ails you but your gout."

A wave of relief swept through me at this suggestion, for I could think of nothing worse than Tobald mourning and moaning and distracting us as we searched for clues. Perhaps it was in Benelaius's mind as well, for he was quick to insist when Tobald demurred.

"Oh, Benelaius, I must go. Grodoveth was under the protection of Ghars, and his death reflects shockingly on our town—and on me as its mayor!"

"Nonsense," said my master. "The mayor cannot help if the king's envoy decides to go off on his own into the middle of a swamp where a murder has recently been committed. Hold yourself blameless and consider the task ahead of you this week. The Merchants' Guild council meets in Ghars, murder or not, and it is up to you and Barthelm to offer them the very best hospitality you can. In order to do that, you must be in the pink of health. Now, have you seen Dr. Braum lately?"

"We stopped at his house," Tobald said, "but he

was out seeing a patient." Then he added under his breath, "That great quack . . . gave me snake dung salve, he did . . . I'd like to snake dung him, I'll tell you. . . ."

"That settles it," Benelaius said, turning to the rest of us. "Captain Flim, Darvik, I would be appreciative if you would lead Lindavar and Jasper to the . . . place of the murder, while I minister to Mayor Tobald."

"Happy to, sir," said Captain Flim, who then corrected himself. "Well, not 'happy to,' the circumstances being what they are, but—"

"No apologies necessary, Captain," my master said. "I understand." He looked at Lindavar and me. "Be my eyes, gentlemen. Mark everything well and let me know in detail what you observe. Farewell, and it was very good to meet you, Mr. Darvik." This with a bow to the gnome.

"The pleasure wor all mine, sor," the gnome said, bowing solemnly. Then he caught himself as Flim had. "Well, not a pleasure, perhaps, circumthingies bein' as they are . . ."

Benelaius smiled as we filed out of the cottage, and I heard him say to Tobald, "Very well, Lord Mayor, please disrobe and I shall examine you."

"Disrobe? But, Benelaius, it's just my great toe . . ."

"What affects the toe may have its source in other parts of the body. The great physician-priest Odum once stated that . . ."

Then the door closed, and we were on our way to the Vast Swamp.

20

Darvik rode behind Flim, I took Jenkus, and Lindavar rode Tobald's mount, a mild and amiable mare. We headed west, passing the Swamp Rat, which, at that hour of the day, appeared to be deserted. A half mile farther, and we were at the spot where I had seen Dovo as the ghost, and where his body had been found.

To my surprise, we turned off the road and trotted down the embankment, riding the same path we had made earlier through the marsh grass and muck. I saw two horses hitched to a dead tree that stood at the swamp's edge.

"This is as far as we can ride," said Captain Flim, dismounting and tying his horse to the tree. We did the same.

"Back in there?" I asked, pointing to what looked like impassable swamp.

"Aye, sor," said Darvik. "Ye'd be surprised, ye would, but ye can step through this swamp even if ye weigh a near ton. Just so's you know where to step."

The little gnome sounded confident, but it was with some trepidation that I followed. Darvik led the way, then Lindavar, me, and Captain Flim bringing up the rear, his hand on his sword hilt. Even though it was daylight, the Vast Swamp was still the Vast Swamp.

We had left our cloaks with the horses, for as soon as you entered the swamp itself, the temperature rose at least ten degrees, the result of all the rotting, all that vegetable death. I could feel the sweat break out on my skin, and hoped that the fluid flowing out of my pores would prevent any of the stench of the swamp from flowing into them.

As nasty as the Vast Swamp is, the worst thing about it is the smell. The reek of decaying vegetation—and other rotting things you'd rather not think about—hangs in the air as heavy mist, and goes up your nostrils and into your sinuses like snakes dipped in acid. It permeates your clothes and your hair as well, even your skin. After a trek through the Vast Swamp, you want to live in the bathtub for a week.

The feel of the swamp beneath your feet isn't too pleasant either. Even the rocks are covered by a shallow layer of marshy soil that your boots press down. When you move on, the footsteps fill up again in seconds. The place was filled with nature's dangers, patches of quicksand and sucking pits that could make a person vanish forever.

All the trees looked dead, even the living ones. Their bark and leaves were black. I wondered if their buds in spring were green, or if even those were black, tinted by the foul sediment pulled up through the roots. Moss festooned their branches, but there was no sense of gaiety in the hangings. They seemed rather to be strips of green, pocked flesh, dangling from decaying corpses. Marsh-reeds picketed the surface, and cattails thrust up like fingers of the drowned. And everywhere the mist drifted, clung, hung, surrounded and claimed us.

"Watch this tree up ahead here, sors," said Darvik softly. "A thornslinger it is. Just move slowly by it, and speak not . . ." I didn't know what a thornslinger was, but its name gave me an idea, and the foot-long thorns that extended from its white, spidery branches gave me a further clue. Needless to say, I did as Darvik suggested.

Suddenly, we came into a large open space, and I looked across what might have been a half mile of sodden marsh, but with few trees. The spaciousness of it was disconcerting, and I hoped we wouldn't have to walk across the expanse. Being in the middle of all that space would make me feel more vulnerable than I had ever felt in my life.

To my relief, Darvik slogged off to the left, and we picked our way around the perimeter of the marshy lake. When we had gone perhaps a hundred yards, he parted a curtain of hanging moss to our left, and we entered the dimness again, leaving the open mere behind. The moss clung to me like wet, filthy hair as I went through the opening, and I continued to wipe my face with my sleeve for several minutes afterward.

At last we saw the two soldiers ahead, standing on top of a small mound that protruded from the swamp like the back of a submerged beast. They tried to look official as we approached, but I could tell that their vigil had been a tense one.

"Anything happen while I was gone?" Captain Flim asked, and one of the soldiers shook his head.

"Not a thing, sir, except . . . well, we did as you commanded and searched farther back in the cave, and . . . we found something, sir."

"The killer?" Lindavar asked.

The soldier got a funny look on his face. "I hope not, sir."

Captain Flim wasn't a man who liked riddles. He pushed past the soldier and descended the stone stairs. We followed, lighting the lanterns we had brought. The steps were slimy, so we trod slowly, and twenty steps downward brought us to the floor of the cave. There was a small chamber there. Its walls were stone, and the striations showed how the levels of rock had been deposited many centuries ago, rock so hard that it stood against the encroachment of the Vast Swamp even to this day.

The floor was stone as well, except for where pockets of moisture had eroded it into a sickly claylike substance. The stone was gray, but the place where Grodoveth had bled away his heart's blood was a flat brown-red. It was the second beheaded corpse I had seen, and much more gruesome than the first. Unlike Dovo's decapitation, this one had been far from efficient.

Instead of the axe striking him in the fleshy part of the neck, the blade had hit on the left shoulder and had torn through part of Grodoveth's collarbone before taking off his head. The blow had continued downward, and the top part of Grodoveth's right shoulder was still attached to the head and neck. The torso was equally hideous to look upon, with a huge gash that had nearly severed the right arm as well as the neck. I could see the spongy interior of the lung.

"Has anything been touched?" Lindavar asked, and the soldiers shook their heads. "Darvik?" he asked the gnome, who was standing halfway down the steps, as though afraid to descend.

"No, sor. I just saw the dead man and I run. Never

even made it all the way down." He gave an apologetic half smile. "Still don't care to, sor."

An axe lay on the floor against the wall, several yards from the body, and Lindavar and I knelt to examine it. There was no doubt that it was the murder weapon, for it was coated with fresh blood and bits of gore. It was much larger and heavier than the one that Dovo had been carrying and that had killed him. The iron was rusty, but the blade still appeared to be very sharp. Near the top of the curved blade, there was a spot where the rust was chipped away and the blade was dulled, and I pointed it out to Lindavar.

He nodded. "Looks as though it's been hit against stone, or possibly strong armor," he said, though I knew of no armor that could have turned a blow struck from that axe. "Do you see any marks of hands upon it?" he asked me, turning it over so that we could see both sides of the handle.

I shook my head but pointed to several marks on the handle. The first was on the inner part of the handle near the blade. It was a deep gouge that had been dug into it, and recently, for the wood exposed was untouched by the grime of years. There were two other marks, one in the center of the blade, and one near the end, as though the axe had been in a wall holder for many years. But no finger marks were visible on the wood.

"Perhaps the killer wore gloves," said Lindavar, and I thought it highly likely.

We straightened up and looked around the small chamber. Except for the now—extinguished torch that Darvik had mentioned, there was nothing of note save for the layers of stone. As I casually looked at the roll of years that they represented, I thought that one layer gleamed more than the others in the lantern light. Greater porosity, I fancied, and wondered how many years it had taken for that inch-wide layer to be deposited, and what creatures had walked Faerûn in that bygone age.

I was about to touch it, as though the contact would make me see in my mind's eye the behemoths of that long-ago eon, when suddenly Captain Flim appeared from around a dark corner, startling me.

"I think you should see this," he said, beckoning with his blazing torch. His face looked somber, almost pale.

We followed him down a twenty-foot tunnel that had long ago been cut by water, for its sides were smooth, with no trace of a stonemason's tools. We had to crouch as we walked, and it was with relief that we came into a chamber larger than the first, so large in fact that Captain Flim's torch and our lanterns only partially illuminated it.

There seemed to be a dais of some kind at the far end, and we walked slowly toward it, the only sound the scrape of our shoes and the dripping of water from the roof of the vault onto the stone floor. I gasped as I saw what sat on that dais, in a massive chair of rotting wood and rusted iron, whose cushions and cloths had long ago moldered away.

The skeleton of a giant seemed to look down at us from empty eye sockets. It was clad in rusted armor, bony forearms still resting on the arms of its rotting throne, fingers curled clawlike over the ends. Its jaw hung down onto the yellow shaft of its neck, and a helm sat lopsided on the bare dome of its skull. On its feet were what was left of its boots, leather strips through which the ivory toe bones peeked. The smell of death had long since vanished. Only dampness and the chill of the grave remained.

Runes were carved on the wall above the seated

skeleton, two lines and then a single word. I started to speak to Lindavar but had to clear my throat before the words would come. "Do you . . . can you read it?"

The wizard nodded, and when he spoke, I heard awe in his tone. "The runes say, 'Bought with blood. Paid for with blood.' And then the name.

" 'Fastred,' " Lindavar read. "This is Fastred's tomb."

21

"Fastred?" said Captain Flim. "The ancient brigand? The ghost?"

"None other," said Lindavar, still gazing as if hypnotized at the seated relic.

"Gods save us," muttered Flim. "Maybe Mayor Tobald was right. Maybe the ghost did it—did for both of them."

"Why hasn't he done for us then?" I said, glad that my voice didn't break. In truth, I was scared. I expected to see the skeleton leap up any second, run down the passageway for his axe, and behead all of us tomb despoilers. "He looks like he hasn't gone anywhere for, oh, at least five hundred years. Give or take a decade," I added lightly to try to keep my fear at bay.

"That is true," said Lindavar. "We're dealing with some physical body here. Among the undead, a ghost might madden its victim or age him ten years; a lich might paralyze his victim; and I have never heard of a wight using a weapon. So wherever this one's spirit now dwells, I greatly doubt that it lies within anything that swings an axe, in spite of its habits in life."

That made me think of something. "Lindavar," I said, "why wouldn't Fastred's axe be with him? Wasn't it the custom in the old times for warriors to be put to rest with their weapons in hand for the next world?"

"So one might think," said Lindavar. He stepped toward the dais then and stopped a foot away, examining the skeleton's hands. "But that appears not to be the case with this burial. I see no sign that any axe has ever rested here."

"I've got another question," said Captain Flim. "What I want to know is, there's supposed to be a treasure here, and what those runes said makes me think that even more. So where is it?"

Lindavar looked at a spot by Fastred's bony feet, just off the dais. There was a square approximately one foot deep by a foot and a half wide that was free of the dark dampness that clung to the rest of the stone floor. "It *was* there, I expect. I also expect that whoever killed Grodoveth also helped himself to the treasure."

Captain Flim dubiously eyed the small bare space where a box had sat. "That's all the bigger it was? I thought Fastred's treasure was supposed to be more, somehow."

"Perhaps he had it all changed to precious gems," I suggested. "You can hold a king's ransom in the palm of your hand that way. Besides, Fastred doesn't seem to have been the showy type. I mean, look at this place—a chair, a brief message, and possibly a treasure. The soul of efficiency. Makes sense to boil all the gold and silver down to a box of jewels."

"Maybe the gnome took it," Flim said frowning.

"Took it and hid it before he came and got us. Maybe he even killed Grodoveth and made up his story when he saw us."

"I doubt if there is a gnome in all of Faerûn," said Lindavar, "capable of beheading a chap the size of Grodoveth. And if you had caught him, why wouldn't he have had the jewel box with him?"

While Lindavar was giving Darvik an alibi, I was examining the floor. "There's another thing," I said, straightening up. "I believe Darvik when he says he never went any farther than the stairs. The footprints are messed up, since your two soldiers were blundering around in here first, Captain, but there's enough for me to see no prints of shoes the size of Darvik's. He's got a much smaller foot than any of us, you know."

"Can you see the footprints of the killer? The one who stole the treasure?" Captain Flim asked. I think he seemed more concerned about the missing cash than the murder of the king's envoy.

"Lindavar's and my footprints are the only ones here, but there is another . . . blurred though . . ." Then I saw a depression in one of the puddles of loamy clay. It was deep, and though it had retained none of the details of the shoe that had trodden in it, not even the size, I thought it might have marked the man's general weight. But the only way to know for sure was to tread in it myself and see how far down my foot went. I sighed and stepped into it.

It went perhaps only half as deep as the previous foot that had stepped into it. "It was a large man," I said.

"Or woman," Lindavar corrected, and I nodded.

"Or woman. And that's about all."

But that wasn't all. As I looked down at the indentation, I glimpsed a bit of white on the floor nearby.

Kneeling, I saw that it was a small amount of chalky powder. Some granules were larger than others, though none were greater than one-sixteenth of an inch. I touched my finger to it, tasted it, and spat it out. It was neither sugar nor salt but tasted bitter. I swept it onto a piece of paper I had brought for making notes, folded it tightly, and put it back into my pocket.

"Find something?" Lindavar asked.

"Powder. Benelaius might want to examine it."

We searched the floor of the chamber but found nothing else. Back at the bottom of the stairs, Captain Flim turned to Lindavar. "Is there anything else you want to do, or can we bundle up the body?"

Lindavar glanced at me and I shrugged. "I think we've seen enough, Captain," Lindavar said.

"All right then, we'll take it back to Suzail for burial. Shall we take that axe along too?"

"Please, and lock it up as evidence."

The soldiers wrapped Grodoveth's corpse in a thin but strong canvas. I didn't envy their toting that dead weight back through the swamp to the road. As we went up the stairs, I looked curiously at the trapdoor, wondering about the mechanism of it.

When we investigated it, we found it to be quite simple, really. One dug one's hand down through the moss, and there, two inches below, was a latch. You just lifted it, and the door would open. No lock was necessary, for I (and probably Fastred) could not imagine anyone stumbling upon the place, unless he knew precisely where to go.

And that posed another question. How did Grodoveth know where to go in the first place? How did he end up at the tomb, and at the mercy of the killer?

The trek back through the swamp was even longer

than the march in. We had to move more slowly so that we wouldn't leave the corpse-bearing soldiers behind. And I finally learned how the thornslinger got its name.

It happened when one of the soldiers slipped in the muck. We had all been walking as quietly as possible, but when the soldier slid off the path, going up to his knees in vile black swamp water, he cursed. Not loudly, and certainly not the worst curse I had ever heard, but enough so that the rest of us turned to see what was wrong, and saw the low-lying tree nearby shiver. One of the limbs twitched violently, like a hand flicking off some unwanted liquid.

But instead of liquid, a dozen foot-long thorns came flying toward the soldiers. Most of them whizzed by, one coming within inches of the second man. But one thorn, with a wet, ugly sound, sank its entire length into the body of Grodoveth. The two soldiers just stared at it, and the one who had fallen scuttled back onto the path and picked up his end of the dropped burden. Both of them shuffled through the muck as quickly as they could, heeding Darvik's frantic but silent gestures.

When our party was far enough away, Darvik halted. "I think yore men had better pull that thorn out the body, sor," he said to Captain Flim.

"Pull it out? Now?" Flim said, no doubt wondering why it could not be done later.

"Aye, sor. Else there won't be a great much of the body to send to Suzail, sor."

Captain Flim raised his eyebrows at that, and ordered the soldiers to unwrap the corpse. Sure enough, the flesh had started to blacken and putrefy around the spot where the thorn had gone in. "Take it out!" Flim ordered, and the soldiers hopped to.

"Try not to get it against yer skin, sors," the gnome

cautioned, and the soldiers' haste slackened considerably.

Soon the thorn was out and thrown off the path. As it sank into the bog, I wondered what effect it might have on a living man, and decided I was lucky not to know. When the corpse was wrapped again, we went on.

I don't recall ever being as glad to set foot on dry land again, even if that land was parched by drought. The contrast between the swamp and the hard, moistureless soil of the rest of the land around Ghars was extraordinary. Some had suggested diverting moisture from the swamp to the surrounding farmlands, but when those budding engineers were asked if they would want to eat grain and vegetables that had been irrigated with water from the Vast Swamp, their faces told the story clearly enough. At the very least, it was felt the swamp water was poisonous, and at the worst, it would turn any drinker reptilian within days, though that's a bit exaggerated. I suspect it would take at least a month.

Captain Flim and the soldiers headed back to town with the body, Darvik started back to his holdings on foot, and Lindavar and I returned to Benelaius's cottage. We discussed the situation as we rode but kept most of our thoughts to ourselves, waiting to share them with Benelaius.

22

As my master opened the door for us, he called up the stairs, "You may get dressed now, Lord Mayor. Your clothes are hanging on the hook just outside the door." He looked at us and gave a tolerant smile. "Mayor Tobald, though usually a jolly sort, doesn't care at all for my examinations. But when someone is in the state he is in, I feel I must be thorough. But come, sit, and tell me what you've seen in the swamp."

Lindavar looked down at our swamp-saturated selves. "May we change first, Benelaius?"

"Oh, of course, of course! Silly of me not to notice. That must be quite uncomfortable, all that squishing around inside your trousers. Yes, do change, and put your dirty clothing down the chute in the hall. But let's just wait a moment until Tobald comes down."

In a few minutes, a miserable Mayor Tobald descended our stairs, cats scurrying from beneath his limping feet. He looked as though he had lost his best friend and a great deal of sleep besides. I decided then that I would never seek public office, no doubt relieving the populace, had they but known.

"Lord Mayor, I regret the comprehensiveness of my examination of you, but I am pleased to say that everything seems to be in order save for your gout. The proper palliative will take a day for me to make, but I shall send Jasper into town first thing tomorrow morning with the tablets to relieve your suffering."

"Thank you, Benelaius," Tobald said. Then he impatiently turned to Lindavar and me. "And out there—did you find anything? Anything to tell us who did this monstrous crime?"

"Two things we know for sure," Lindavar said. "The first is that Grodoveth was beheaded in the same manner as Dovo, and the second is that no one will ever have to seek the tomb of Fastred again."

For a moment, Tobald seemed stricken dumb. Then he said, "Fastred's tomb? You found Fastred's tomb?"

"Grodoveth did," I said. "Or maybe his killer did. At any rate, whatever treasure was there is gone."

"Quite fascinating," said Benelaius briskly. "I shall have to visit it sometime. Now, Tobald, I think it would be best were you to ride home and rest that foot."

"No rest, no rest," said Tobald. "Too much to do for tomorrow."

"Give yourself some time at least," said my master, "before throwing yourself back into your work. And retire early tonight. No drinking at the Bold Bard."

"Very well, Benelaius." Tobald looked at the wizard with pleading eyes. "You *will* find this killer, won't you? Just to know that this fiend is still at large . . ."

"We shall certainly do our best. Now let Jasper

assist you in mounting your horse." I raised my eyebrows, but no one noticed.

Tobald was not an easy man to fling into the saddle, but I got it accomplished. We stood and watched him ride away, his shoulders hunched, his head down. I felt sorry for him, losing a friend, seeing his town dishonored by allowing an envoy of the king to get murdered, and of course, having to put on a cheery countenance for the arrival of the guild bigwigs the next day. Even though the job was primarily ceremonial, a mayor's lot was not always a happy one.

"I am very concerned about Mayor Tobald," said Benelaius quietly, when Tobald had ridden out of earshot. "He is quite naturally upset, but I fear there is more to it than that. I even tested his blood, and extracted . . . this."

From the folds of his robe he produced a small vial that contained a few drops of a pale yellow liquid. "I have already analyzed a small amount, but I should like you to confirm my findings, Lindavar. First, however, you and Jasper should get out of those wet things."

Lindavar and I went upstairs and changed, putting our muddy clothes down the chute that dropped them into a basket in the kitchen. Back downstairs, Benelaius led the way into his study, where a long and wide bench held a number of wizardly and scientific instruments. Lindavar, in spite of the unfamiliar surroundings, performed the procedure unerringly. I suppose one alembic's pretty much like another when you know what to do with it.

The younger mage added a drop of some reagent from the rows of multicolored vials on shelves above the bench, then fitted the vial securely into a centrifuge. He pumped the foot pedals to spin the device for several minutes, then drew a precipitate out of the vial and placed it on a glass slide. To it he added several drops of other chemicals, under whose influence it turned a variety of unpleasant shades. Finally Lindavar straightened up and looked grimly at Benelaius.

"Blackweed," he said, and Benelaius nodded. "When this enters the system," Lindavar went on, "it will kill in twenty-four hours."

"Don't worry," Benelaius said. "We're in time. I . . . gave him something for it. He doesn't know."

"But who would want to poison Mayor Tobald?" I asked. As far as I was concerned, the mayor was inoffensive and ineffectual. What threat could he be to anyone?

"And who would want to kill Dovo or Grodoveth?" Benelaius said. "Yet killed they were. Now," he went on, walking toward the door of the study, "I should like to hear your reports of what you found at this . . . tomb, was it? And if I'm not wrong, I do believe it's past time for our noonday meal."

I cooked a hearty luncheon of soup, which I served with black bread, and while we ate we told Benelaius everything we had seen that morning in the swamp. He looked at each of us intently as we spoke, and I fancied that each word, each disparate observation on our part was coalescing in his mighty brain, forming some ingenious solution that he would soon share with us.

When I came to the part about finding the white powder on the tomb floor, I handed the bit of paper to him. He unwrapped it, wet his finger, and tasted the powder the way I had in the cave. His lip curled for an instant at its bitterness, and he grunted and wrapped it up again.

"We'll analyze this after lunch," he said, putting it in one of his inner pockets.

Lindavar and I finished our story, and I leaned forward breathlessly, waiting to see what conclusions

Benelaius would draw. "So," he said slowly, wiping his mouth and beard with his napkin, "it seems that Grodoveth was beheaded by a left-handed killer at Fastred's tomb. But the question remains, what was he doing at Fastred's tomb in the first place?"

Lindavar steepled his fingers and looked at the inside of them as he spoke. "He was reading about Fastred in the library."

"But *before* the ghost started appearing," I reminded him.

"Yes. But supposing that was merely a coincidence. Then, as Dovo began to appear as the ghost, Grodoveth got more interested, more curious. The more he reads, the more he starts to discover about Fastred, where his tomb might be, and the treasure that's supposed to be there as well.

"Then Dovo is found murdered, and it becomes more than a treasure hunt for Grodoveth. Despite his faults, he is the king's envoy, and he sees a chance to bring a killer to justice. Find the tomb, he reasons, and he may also find the person who kills as Fastred killed—and a treasure to boot.

"So, by using clues that he found in the old books, Grodoveth is actually able to discover not only the whereabouts of the tomb, but the secret of opening it as well."

"Would that be possible?" I interjected. "I mean, weren't these bandit kings usually able to keep their tombs a secret? You know, the old 'dead men tell no tales' thing?"

"Since you found no skeletons of those who had interred Fastred," Benelaius said, "I think it likely that *someone* put him in there and left alive. Perhaps his curse kept those who knew the secret away from the tomb."

"But it didn't keep them from talking about the

tomb," said Lindavar, "at least elliptically, if someone—
the killer or Grodoveth or maybe both—was able to
find and open it."

"Mmm," Benelaius said. "So you think Grodoveth
and possibly the killer put together the different clues
left hither and yon over the years and found the tomb."

"Yes," Lindavar said. "Unfortunately when
Grodoveth found it, the killer was lying in wait and
killed him."

"Or," I said, "perhaps the killer hadn't found the
tomb at all but followed Grodoveth there, killed him,
and took the treasure."

Lindavar considered that for a moment and then
nodded. "True," he said. "We have no knowledge of
anyone else examining those particular books in the
library."

"The lack of something proves nothing," said
Benelaius. "The killer might have gotten the information elsewhere. With all due respect to Phelos
Marmwitz, there are greater receptacles of knowledge than the Ghars library. For example, I'd be willing to wager that my own modest collection contains
enough works of local folklore and history for a
methodical reader to locate Fastred's tomb." He
sighed. "Be that as it may, do you two feel that we are
any closer to an actual solution now than we were
before?"

"Further away, if anything," Lindavar said. "Before,
Grodoveth was strongly in the lead as the murderer,
but becoming a victim has definitively put him out of
the running."

"Oh, I don't know," I said flippantly. "Perhaps he
was the killer, and out of guilt, he chopped his own
head off."

Neither Benelaius nor Lindavar laughed. Instead
they looked at me with pained expressions, and I

realized my joke had not been terribly funny. "Sorry," I said.

"Apology accepted," said Benelaius. "Well, we must press on. Any suggestions?"

"Why don't I go back to town?" I said. "This murder has brought us full circle back to the phony ghost again. If Grodoveth had been killed in his room at the Swamp Rat, or on the road to town, or nearly anywhere else, there would be no further connection with the ghost. But to have him slain in Fastred's tomb . . . well, if nobody had taken the treasure, I'd have thought the actual ghost killed him. So my idea is, learn more about the ghost, learn more about the murderer. They seem inextricably bound."

"And exactly how are you going to learn about . . . the ghost?" asked Benelaius.

"By talking to everyone who saw Dovo playing it. I have the list. Maybe there's something that one of the witnesses remembers that might shed some light on this whole murky business. I swear, it's getting muddier than the Vast Swamp itself."

"Muddy . . ." said Benelaius. "Very well, Jasper, go to town. But that 'muddy' business reminds me . . . before you go, please do the washing. It's a breezy day at last, so it should dry quickly, and Lindavar has brought only a limited wardrobe."

I bet Camber Fosrick never had to do the laundry before he went off investigating, I thought as I trudged into the kitchen.

23

The dirty garments lay at the bottom of the chute from upstairs, and I had to remove several cats who were reclining on the unmuddied parts of the clothes, which were few. I scraped soap into the washtub, filled it with boiling water, and washed the clothes.

It was extraordinary, I thought, how the swamp muck from Lindavar's and my clothing had permeated everything else in the clothes pile, even Benelaius's robe of the night before. But some hard work and elbow grease soon had them spotless, and I threw out the soapy water and rinsed them in fresh.

At last I had the clothes hanging on the line, and bade good-bye to Benelaius and Lindavar, who were now at work in the study, examining, I hoped, the powder I had found. I left them to their task and headed for Ghars.

It was midafternoon when I arrived, and though I hoped that I would be able to speak to everyone I could and return before dark, I doubted it would happen. Benelaius had given me money for lodging were I too uneasy to return home at night, but Jenkus had outdistanced pursuers before, and there was no reason he could not do so again.

I stopped first at the library, where I asked Mr. Marmwitz if he could recall anyone but Grodoveth looking into the past history of Fastred. "Alas, not for years," he said, shaking his head. Nonetheless, I looked on the flyleaves of most of the books to see if there was any record of withdrawal in recent months.

Marmwitz was correct. The most recent withdrawal had been eight years before, and the patron had been Mrs. Barnabas Hinkel, who had been dead and in the ground for seven of those years.

Back on the street, I got out my list, concentrating on it and trying to ignore the flood of people listening to Barthelm Meadowbrock's commands. It was difficult. They were scurrying all about me, hanging banners welcoming the Merchants' Guild council, putting up garlands and wreaths on the lampposts, washing the windows of all the store fronts, even sweeping the horse dung out of the gutters. Shabby, sleepy little Ghars was undergoing a metamorphosis, but I was paying it no mind.

The first two names on my ghost witness list were easy. Dovo was dead, and the Arabel merchant was probably back in Arabel. I scratched them off. The next was trickier—Mayor Tobald. At this point I figured the last thing he needed was more talk about ghosts.

Looking up the street, I spotted him standing next to Barthelm, disobeying Benelaius's orders to rest before throwing himself back into the fray. Tobald was looking upward and signaling with his hands, apparently guiding some garland or banner hanger lost in the shuffle. No, it might be best to leave the mayor to his civic pleasures and go farther down the list.

Diccon Piccard had seen the Dovo-ghost on the twenty-seventh of Kythorn, so I tied up Jenkus and went over to his jewelry shop on Wattle Lane. The heavy wooden door reinforced with steel bands was open, and through it came the sound of the Selgaunt fiddle that Piccard played whenever he was not assisting a customer. I think the tune was either "Warrior's Woe" or "Red-haired Lad"—most fiddle tunes sound the same to me.

When Diccon Piccard saw me, he called out my name as though he were delighted I was entering his shop, though I had never bought a thing from him and could ill afford to. His smile was as wide as the Dragonmere, and his great bush of hair was blindingly white.

"Jasper, is it not! Benelaius's man! And a finer man is hard to imagine! Benelaius is very lucky indeed!" Diccon Piccard was a born salesman. I had no doubt that if he used that much oil on people who could afford his wares, the precious jewels practically waltzed out of his shop.

"Greeting, Diccon Piccard," I said. "You must be prepared for the arrival of the guild leaders, if you have time to play so beautifully." Actually, he didn't play all that well, but this flattery stuff becomes mutual pretty quickly.

We went back and forth for a while, and when we touched on the subject of the newest murder (which made him frown for only a second, for he had not known Grodoveth) I was finally able to come to the subject at hand. "Ah, yes, the ghost," he said with a smile, as though Dovo's had been a noble jest. "I don't mind telling you that it gave me a fright, quite a fright it did, even though it *was* a hoax. When I saw that dreadful apparition, I went shivery all over. We rode away as fast as our horses would take us."

" 'We?' " I said. "You weren't alone?"

He looked guilty, as though he had just betrayed a trust. "I, uh . . . oh bother, I said I wouldn't tell. . . ."

"Surely, sir, civic duty is more important than a secret held for a friend. I assure you that no one but my master and I shall know, that is, unless it should prove absolutely necessary to capture the killer."

"All right then, I was riding back from the Swamp Fox with Barthelm."

"Barthelm Meadowbrock?"

"Yes. We had gone out there together just to see what the place was like—and I wasn't impressed. But he didn't want anyone to know he was out there, for he feared that if Shortshanks found he was patronizing another tavern, the dwarf would not be cooperative in filling Barthelm's spirits order for the guild meeting. So I let on that I was alone when I saw the ghost . . . er, Dovo."

"Perfectly understandable, Diccon Piccard. And I thank you for your honesty."

"You are quite welcome, Jasper. My honesty also extends to my business dealings, so I trust if you ever require my services, say a fine stone for a beloved young lady, or . . ." And so it went until I was able to extricate myself.

Elizabeth Clawthorn, known to everyone as Looney Liz, was next on the list, but since she lived just south of Ghars, I decided to make her my last stop on the way home. That meant Lukas Spoondrift was next.

I didn't look forward to seeing Spoondrift. He was my former employer at the Sheaf of Wheat, and hadn't taken it very well when I had left his miserable job to go with Benelaius. Add to that fact the certainty that he was going to be as busy as anyone in Ghars getting ready for tomorrow's guild visit, and I knew I would have a none too happy host for my own call.

Spoondrift was a fat hulk of a man, who ate up much of his own profits. But he could afford it, especially with the income the Merchants' Guild meeting would bring. Barthelm Meadowbrock was spending a great deal of his own money to host the event, and the guild leaders themselves could be counted on to spend a great deal.

The inn owner was outside, overseeing the unloading of the butcher's wagon, carefully counting each fowl, fish, beef and lamb quarter as it crossed his kitchen threshold. He stopped and examined some of the butchered beasts, as though he feared spoilage, though Butcher Skedmoor's reputation was unsullied. The butcher stood by, frowning every time Spoondrift slowed his men in their unloading.

I waited until the last carcass was out of the wagon and the voucher was signed. When Spoondrift started to go back into his kitchen, I left the security of the barrels behind which I'd been standing and walked up to him.

"Mr. Spoondrift," I said, "could I have a word with you?"

When he saw who I was, his face grew even colder than before. Too much time in the meat lockers, I thought. "A word with me, slop boy?"

"I'm not a slop boy anymore, sir," I spoke with as much dignity as a former slop boy could muster. "I work for the wizard Benelaius, as you know."

" 'As you know,' " he parroted. "Well, don't we speak high and mighty now. Where'd you get all that education, slop boy?"

"My master has tutored me," I said, trying to keep

my temper. My right buttock will forever bear a scar from one of Spoondrift's beatings.

"Isn't that nice," he said sarcastically, "that some employers have the time to educate their servants. Have no time for such shenanigans myself. I'm running an inn here, not a school."

I could see the conversation was getting nowhere fast, so I tried to butter up the old weasel. "Nevertheless, I learned a great deal by working here, sir. Invaluable lessons about life." Like how to avoid working in future for a scum-swilling swine like Spoondrift.

"What do you want?" he barked.

"As you might have heard, I'm trying to aid my master by finding out certain things about the recent murders outside of Ghars."

"Ah, the slop boy's become the great Camber Fosrick now, has he?"

I made myself smile. "Hardly that. But I would like to know about your experience when you came across Dovo as the ghost."

"Look, sonny, if you really want to know who killed Dovo and the envoy, all you've got to do is ask me."

I had no idea things were going to be this easy. "All right," I said. "Who do you think did it?"

"I don't think, I *know*. It was that roofer's son, that Rolf. He's got a temper hotter than a midsummer desert at high noon, he's in love with Barthelm's daughter, and both Dovo and the envoy made insulting advances to her. Now they're both dead. And where was he while they were getting murdered, eh? If I were you, Mr. Jasper Fosrick, that's what I'd be finding out, and not asking a lot of stupid questions about phony ghosts. Now run along and play your little games. I've got work to do." And he went into the inn, slamming shut the kitchen door behind him.

If it was going to be that simple, I was going to be very annoyed. And the thing that galled me was that it could be just that simple. A lad filled with a jealous, killing rage who sets out to avenge his sweetheart's honor.

Still, Rolf was right-handed, but maybe we were wrong. Maybe he had come up behind Dovo and Grodoveth. No one kept track of Rolf when he wasn't working. He could have been out on the swamp road the night Dovo was killed, and he could have followed Grodoveth early that morning to the tomb, and gone away with the treasure. Maybe the thing to do was watch and see if Rolf started buying drinks for the house.

Behind me I heard footsteps, and turned to see Butcher Skedmoor coming up behind me. His men had finished watering their horses, and they were ready to take their wagon back to their shop. "A word, young man," said the butcher, and I nodded respectfully. "One thing you ought to know before paying owt to what old Spoondrift says—he dislikes the lad, y'see. Rolf, I mean. Had a new roof put on part of the inn six months back, waited too long, the old roof leaked and damaged some joists beneath. Young Rolf's got the wood shingles up on the roof, leaves boxes of them there overnight, and around midnight, *crack*! Their weight breaks the rotten beams beneath, and the boxes of shingles come crashing through the roof, through the attic floor, and shingles start raining onto the bed of Spoondrift and his missus.

"Well, Spoondrift makes a great stink." Butcher Skedmoor snickered. "More than usual for the bean-eating old mole. But Rolf says that the wood was already bad, so he can't be blamed, and Spoondrift says that he shouldn't've had all that weight on the roof, and so it goes. Finally Rolf's father says they'll share the cost of rebuilding the floors and roof, but that's not good enough for Spoondrift, who should've had his roof fixed years before. They're still arguing before the magistrate in Wheloon. Anyways, lad, that's why you should maybe take that story with a grain of salt—or a box of shingles."

I thanked the butcher, and he waved a pleasant good-bye as his wagon creaked away. His story didn't clear Rolf, but at least it gave a reason for Spoondrift's malevolence.

I sighed and looked at my list. I would get no more out of Lukas Spoondrift. Farmer Bortas was next, but I had already talked to him. Bryn Goldtooth, the halfling, was the last on the list, except for myself, and I headed over to his shop.

24

Bryn Goldtooth was getting ready to close up for the day. He was not involved in the furious preparations that occupied the other inhabitants of Ghars, since he was not a member of the Merchants Guild. His shop was a buy-and-sell-and-trade place where you either found exactly what you were looking for, or nothing at all. It was a labyrinth of dimly lit narrow aisles, where a stuffed leucrotta head might sit between a pair of gold candlesticks and an assortment of used cranial drills.

And since his stock came from his customers rather than from wholesale merchants, he felt no sense of brotherhood with the guild. Besides, it would have curdled his halfling blood to give money to human merchants and receive nothing in return except an intangible membership.

While I had never patronized Diccon Piccard, I had bought things from Bryn Goldtooth. I think he gave me better prices because I had told him about my halfling blood. No purchase or trade was ever made without his looking up at me, winking, and saying, "We halflings have to stick together, eh?"

But he showed no mercy on full-blooded humans. He lived to outbargain them, and when one left his shop dejected, having lost the best of a deal, his day was made. Apparently he had had a good day, for he greeted me cheerily and didn't even look disappointed when I told him I had not come on business but to ask him about his recent experience with Dovo.

He laughed merrily. "I can't tell you a single thing about that, my boy! When I saw that man standing there with his glowing face and his swinging axe, I wasn't going to hang around. I just booted Bupkin in the side and we tore off down the road, and I didn't look back until I was safe in Ghars."

"That seems to have been the reaction of most people, including me," I said, unashamed to admit it.

"All but one," Goldtooth said. "Looney Liz."

"Elizabeth Clawthorn? I was going to go and visit her."

"You do that. All us sane people light out, we see a ghost. But old Liz was too crazy to run, she was. Least that's what she said when she come in here trying to trade a dead cat for a linen tablecloth. Needless to say, I didn't make the trade. 'Course maybe she didn't run because she's too ancient. Can you imagine that old crone going any faster than her usual creep?"

"Did she see any more than we did?"

"You ask her about it on your way home. Maybe it was just another one of her stories. She's a queer one—sometimes she seems as right as rain, and other times you'd swear she's got a turnip in her head instead of a brain. Speaking of turnips, I took half a bushel in trade today. Now I don't know if you're a turnip eatin' man, but I could make you a deal. . . ."

As it happened, I was not a turnip eating man, and got out after spending only three copper pieces on a two-year-old journal that happened to have an installment of a Camber Fosrick story I had never read. Unfortunately it was the third of four, so I had no idea what came before or how the mystery would end, not unlike my present situation.

The sky was beginning to darken, so I hastened south out of Ghars. A mile's ride brought me to the small, ramshackle cottage where Liz Clawthorn lived. Set far back from the road, the house was badly in need of paint, and greasy hides covered the window openings. Wreaths of dead flowers decorated the door and walls, their long stems twisted into eerie shapes, and a dead dog lay under a withered tree. I wondered if she would try to trade it to Bryn Goldtooth.

There was a small garden to the side of the house, where Looney Liz grew vegetables and potatoes, but the tomatoes had died on the vines, and the lettuces were brown and sparse from the drought. How, I wondered, did she manage to live?

I tied Jenkus to a dead apple tree and went up to the door and knocked. It was for politeness only since the door hung from one hinge like an idiot's grin.

"Who comes, who comes?" the woman croaked from inside. The door stuttered open, and Liz Clawthorn smiled at me from a row of teeth either yellow, blackened, or missing altogether. As short as I am, she was far shorter, nearly dwarven in size, though a human. A smock that might have been washed the winter before covered her from neck to feet, and her long, filthy hair hid all but the unpleasant features of her face.

I had once asked Benelaius if he thought she was a

witch, but he had shaken his head gently. "Nay. A poor woman with wandering wits, and that is all." And though there were some who would disagree with him, I daresay he was right.

But this day it appeared that Liz Clawthorn was having one of her more lucid spells. She came up to me as though she had trouble making out the details of my face, and then, to my great surprise, she actually recognized me. "Ah, 'tis Jasper," she said. "Benelaius's lad. Come in, come in, come out of the foul death air." I didn't know what she meant, for the air inside was far fouler than that outside.

I entered and gave her the bag of vegetables and the loaf of bread I had brought for her. "A gift for you, Mother Clawthorn," I said, and her smile grew broader.

"A good lad you are, Jasper, and I thank you. Sit you down." She held up a bunch of carrots. "Fine oranges," she proclaimed, then set the bundle of produce on a worn and dirty table. "Now have ye come for truth or lies or tea? I have no tea, but I have the others."

"Truth, I think, Mother," I said, playing her game.

"You always were a good son to me, Jamie," she said, and I immediately decided not to call her mother again. "So I'll tell ye true." Ah. Well, in that case, 'Mother' would she be.

"You saw a man dressed as the ghost of Fastred some time back, didn't you, Mother Clawthorn? The man named Dovo?"

"I saw the ghost itself, not some Dobo. It was the ghost of Fastred, but when I saw it, Jamie, I thought it was your father, yes, rest his soul, the ghost of your poor father. He swung an axe, yes, the way your poor father did when he cut down the tree, you know, the one with the rope that you would swing on when you were little. And I thought he was after me, I did, and I run away at first, but then I remembered that I never did tell him about that bucket and how it had a hole and to mend it before he got water, so I went back, I did, and then I saw him with his golden hand.

"Your father, Jamie, never had a golden hand, so I knew it was a ghost. And he went on into the swamp, and I followed him, I did, and then he stopped and I stopped too because I knew if he saw me there then he would eat me, and I didn't want to get et, so I hid and was quiet and watched him."

Her eyes widened, staring into the middle distance, and I knew she was seeing what she had seen on that night. "And what did he do?" I asked softly.

"He waved his golden hand," she said, seeing it happen again. "He waved it over and over. And far away across the swamp, another ghost waved back with *his* golden hand, and they waved at each other for a long time. . . ."

"A golden hand?" I said.

"Yes," she said sharply, turning back to me so that I jumped. "I see them all the time, the golden hands. At night they glow, all golden. In the dark. It's getting dark *now*," she said, and I thought I heard menace in her tone. Maybe she was just trying to scare Jamie, wherever and whoever he was. "I'll see the golden hands soon. They come with the moon and the stars."

I talked to her a bit longer, until it grew dark inside the hovel and she lit a candle, to my relief. Harmless or not, I didn't relish sitting in the darkness with the mad old woman.

When I saw that I could get no more out of her, I thanked her for her time and the visit, and rose to leave. "You can't go yet, Jamie," she said.

"I'm Jasper," I reminded her. "Not Jamie."

"Oh," she said, a world of disappointment in the word. "All right then, you must be getting back to Benelaius, I suppose." Her sanity was like a lantern that blinked on and off, and I rose, eager to be on my way.

It was dark when I opened the door, and to the north I saw a wagon coming down the road, a farmer returning home from Ghars. A lantern hung from a pole, and swayed back and forth over his head, illuminating the road ahead.

"A golden hand," said Liz Clawthorn from behind me, and I turned and looked at her.

"What?"

"A golden hand," she said. "There it waves."

I looked back at the wagon, then turned to her again. "Do you see the wagon?" I asked her.

"Wagon? Nay, only the gold hand that waves and waves."

We watched as the wagon passed fifty yards away, and listened to the sound of its wheels, and I realized that Elizabeth Clawthorn's old eyes must be like a cloudy lens, and thought that, to her, a lantern would look like a bright smudge, and its rays, separate golden fingers of light.

A golden hand. A lantern. And another, far away across the swamp.

I bade her good-bye, and she begged a kiss of her "Jamie." I gave her one, though it gave me no pleasure, and went on my way south, toward the swamp road, thinking of the great mere within the swamp, and of lights winking back and forth across it.

25

Dovo must have had a lantern in the swamp on those nights. But what was he looking for? And why would he brave the trek into the swamp to that inner lake near which we found Fastred's tomb?

And most important of all, who was carrying the other lantern?

All these thoughts and more rushed through my head as I neared the turn-off to the left that would put me on the swamp road and take me home to Benelaius's cottage. Indeed, my mind was rushing so that I completely forgot the horror of the night before until I reached the spot where I had seen Dovo playing Fastred's ghost.

Then the terrors of that night and the nightmares it had caused made me bump my heels against Jenkus's sides and urge him to a greater speed than his easy trot provided. He complied, but with a complaining whicker, as though the previous night's chase had never occurred. Animals forget past fears and hurts all too readily. Perhaps that is why they are able to live with our cruelty.

We cantered down the road and past the Swamp Rat, which had only a few horses tied in front of it. I suspected the farmers who patronized it were staying home. What with two savage murders in as many days, I didn't blame them.

Two hundred yards past the Swamp Rat, I thought I heard the pursuing footsteps once again. At first I told myself it was only my imagination, so terrified had I been the night before. But as I listened, trying to transform the sounds into wind through swamp grass or the croaking of bullfrogs, I knew the sound was real, and familiar, and chilling.

da-da-boom . . .

da-da-Boom . . .

da-da BOOM!

Whatever the monstrous thing (or things) was, it was behind me again. But if Jenkus and I had outrun it once, we could outrun it twice.

"Hyah!" I shouted, and Jenkus was off like a shot. I nearly laughed in relief as the menacing sounds fell farther behind. Soon we would be home and safe.

And then Jenkus lost a shoe.

I heard the rattle as it came off. He stumbled, caught himself, and staggered again. Unprepared for the drastic change in speed, I slewed to the left and fell, automatically kicking my feet free of the stirrups so that I would not be dragged. I rolled several feet before coming to a stop. In the darkness, I could not see Jenkus, but what I *could* see as it approached was the thing that had pursued me.

My dream about four riders on four horses had not been very accurate. There were *five* heads approaching me, but they didn't belong to five separate riders. Instead, every reptilian, dagger-toothed head belonged to the single massive body of a hydra, the dragonlike behemoth that slowly but inexorably advanced toward me on four massive and clawed legs, the claws clacking against the ground to be followed a moment later by the impact of the huge leg upon the earth. . . .

da-da-BOOM . . .

I pushed myself to my feet, but Jenkus, coward that he was, was already limping down the road toward home. The monster was less than twenty feet away, and I knew that I could not hope to outrun it. No weapon, no speed, and no future to speak of. If I'd had a mirror, I would have kissed myself good-bye.

Then, behind me, I heard the sound of hoofbeats and thought that perhaps Jenkus was coming back in an equine act of heroism. When I turned to look, I beheld not Jenkus but a lone rider bearing down on me, long sword raised. And then I heard her scream.

Yes, *her*. It was a woman's voice crying out in berserker rage, and I knew it could be none other than Kendra. For an instant that felt like forever I stood there, a frenzied swordswoman attacking on one side, a savage monster thundering up on the other.

Kendra reached me first, but her sword did not descend. Instead, she swept on by me. As I whirled to look, she reined up just as she came abreast of the hydra, and with a single stroke sheared off its closest head.

The other four heads howled as their comrade bounced across the road and over the embankment. Kendra followed her stroke with an instant backswing, and a second head bounded away, separated from a thick, serpentine neck. But before she could prepare for another blow, one of the ghastly heads came down and struck her on the left leg.

Her armor cushioned the blow, but from her grunt of pain and anger, I could tell she had been hurt. The offending head was quickly chastised with another swipe of her sword that nearly separated it from its neck. It hung from an inch-thick strand of leathery flesh, the jaws still snapping impotently.

I would have run to help her but for two things. First, I didn't have a sword, and second, even if I did have one, I wouldn't have known what to do with it. I had no doubt that while I was working on getting the correct grip, one of the remaining heads would have grabbed and held me while the other would have begun to nibble daintily at my tasty flesh.

So I did the next best thing. I picked up whatever rocks I could find in the roadway and started flinging them at the hydra from a safe distance. Admittedly, it was not my most heroic moment, but I blush to admit that it comes close. I think I actually hit one of the heads on my third throw. I might have made it blink.

But Kendra was doing quite nicely without my help. She had by this time closed with the monster's body, and now, batting away the two heads that roared at her like bothersome flies, she sank her sword up to the hilt into the scaly chest.

After that, no more heads needed to be separated from necks. The beast bellowed once (twice, if you count each head as a separate bellow) and fell straight down, its heart pierced. Kendra narrowly escaped being crushed by the beast's descent, but her horse was well trained and had backed off as soon as she had withdrawn her sword.

The thud when the hydra hit the dirt sent up a dust cloud that made the night even darker. The two remaining heads continued to gibber and moan and snap for a while, but by the time the dust settled, they were still, and Kendra was next to me, still mounted, blood dripping from her left thigh.

"So who have I risked my life to save?" she said, looking down at me.

"I'm Jasper," I said. "Benelaius's servant. I saw you the other day in the swamp."

"And," she said, "at the tavern the night before. You were one of the shy ones, if I'm not mistaken."

"Well, if you mean I didn't make any unwanted advances, then yes, I suppose I was indeed one of the shy ones."

"Lucky for you," she said. "If you'd acted like most of your rude sex, I might have let you die."

At first I was about to say, "Oh, you wouldn't have done that," but then I realized she might have done worse than that. I had no proof that she had not been the slayer of both Dovo and Grodoveth. Perhaps this meeting was doubly lucky, not only saving my life, but also giving me the opportunity to question further this beautiful warrior.

"Thank you," I said. "You most definitely saved my life. But you've been wounded. Why not come with me to Benelaius's cottage? He's very skilled at healing, and you can't ride far, bleeding like that."

"This wouldn't have anything to do with the fact that you have to walk back, would it?"

"Milady, I will still walk back next to your horse, if it please you. You've saved my life, and I wish you only the best."

She gave a half-laugh and patted the saddle behind her. "Come up and ride behind me," she said. "Darrun can easily bear us both to your master's house."

Triple good fortune, I thought as I climbed up behind her and she took my hands and placed them around her slim waist so that I would not fall. "Hold tight," she said, "but put your hands only where I placed them if you wish your fingers to remain unbroken. And try not to bump my injured leg."

In spite of holding myself like a statue, I still enjoyed the ride. So tall she was that my face was against her back, and some of her red hair spilled out the back of her helmet so that it brushed my cheek. It was very soft and smelled of spices. But she had been fighting hard, and the scent of her body was musky, though I found it not at all unpleasant. Indeed, I would have been happy to ride on forever with her. Finally she spoke to me.

"You're brave to be riding with me, aren't you? Especially after what Captain Flim thinks of me."

"And what's that?"

"That I killed Dovo for insulting me the other night. And that I probably killed the king's envoy Grodoveth as well, since he was insulting too. And there's further evidence against me."

What was she doing, confessing? "And that is?"

"I was searching for treasure in the Vast Swamp. Grodoveth was killed in Fastred's tomb, and now the treasure is gone. Suspicion should naturally fall on me."

"Do you mind my asking how you heard all this? I mean, assuming of course that you didn't actually kill Grodoveth."

"An adventurer hears nearly everything. And it's my business to know about the things that concern me. Besides, just because the treasure's stolen doesn't mean it's gone. To my way of thinking, it's no crime to steal from a thief."

"Assuming that you didn't take it to begin with, and aren't just saying this to divert suspicion from yourself."

"A possibility. But if I wanted to divert your suspicions from me, there's a far easier way to do it."

"And that is?"

"Kill you the way I killed Dovo and Grodoveth. *If* I killed them in the first place."

I swallowed heavily. "Very true," I said. "My death would very efficiently end my suspicions of you. But if you wanted me dead, I doubt you would have saved my life."

"Sometimes," she said, "one does foolhardy things just for the sheer joy of doing them. Frankly, it's fun to kill monsters."

"And is it fun to get wounded in the process?"

"Perhaps. If you're riding with someone who thinks you capable of killing them. I enjoy that somehow. I suppose it's the bully in me."

"I don't think you would kill me," I said with more bravado than I felt.

"We're not at your home yet, are we?" she said, and I had no answer. I simply clung to her waist, figuring that if she did kill me on the way, I at least had the consolation of embracing her until she did the deed.

26

But when we arrived at Benelaius's cottage I was unscathed, though Kendra seemed weary from the loss of blood. Benelaius and Lindavar were standing outside worriedly, since Jenkus had arrived home alone, and they both hailed us as we came riding up.

"Kendra saved my life," I said as I climbed off her horse. "A hydra attacked me and Jenkus threw a shoe. But Kendra killed the monster."

"With a slight wound to myself, I fear," she said. "Jasper told me you were skilled in the healing arts." She tried to swing her wounded leg over the saddle but could not, and clung to her horse's neck. The three of us came to her rescue immediately, lifting her off her steed and onto the ground, where she leaned heavily on Lindavar and held her left leg aloft.

"That looks quite nasty, my dear," Benelaius said. "But I have no doubt that we can soon set you right."

We helped her inside and onto a large, comfortable chaise before the fire. Benelaius chattered all the while. "A hydra, you say? A common hydra, I suppose. The cryohydra is unknown here, and the pyrohydra is quite rare. Since you are not singed, I assume it was a common multiheaded variety. Not a lernaean hydra either, I wager."

"The kind that regenerate their heads?" Kendra said. "No, this one's heads didn't come back once I lopped them off, thank the gods."

"Must have been very hungry to come out of the swamp," Benelaius went on. "Stupid beasts, though, and slow. Move well in swamps but awkwardly on land. All the better for both of you, eh?"

"Still fast enough to catch my leg," Kendra said as we eased her down. In spite of the pain that caused beads of sweat to appear on her pale and lovely face, she chuckled at the sight of the cats. "Do with me what you will. I trust a man who likes animals."

"Lindavar, please heat water on the stove while I get the salves and unguents. Jasper, see to it that Jenkus and the lady's horse are cared for, then come back here. Quickly now."

I did as my master said, envying him the task of having such a patient as that magnificent specimen of a woman. I wondered if he was as much in awe of Kendra as I was, and assumed he was not. Benelaius was undoubtedly not a creature of his passions. Kendra would be interesting to him only for what she might tell him about the fighting habits of hydrae. I sighed. What a waste of intimacy.

I fed and rubbed down the horses. By the time I went back in, Kendra was sleeping, her wounded leg covered by a virginally white sheet, and Benelaius and Lindavar had just finished putting away the equipment. Benelaius motioned me into his study, where the three of us sat down. He filled a pipe with tobacco and lit it, and his words poured forth on the smoke.

"I have sewn up the wound and given her a sleeping draught," my master said. "By morning she will feel much better, but she should rest here a day or two. She has lost some blood and must regain her strength." He smiled admiringly. "A fine woman, and a brave one, though one who, I fear, would not suffer fools gladly."

"Meaning Dovo and Grodoveth," I suggested.

"I believe they would have qualified as fools," Benelaius said. "Now tell me, Jasper, what you've learned in town today. Did the ghost witnesses prove at all valuable?"

I related everything that I had learned, and was pleased to see that some of the information hit home. Benelaius and Lindavar seemed particularly interested in the fact that Barthelm Meadowbrock was with Diccon Piccard when he saw the disguised Dovo, and their eyebrows raised when I told them Lukas Spoondrift's theory about Rolf being the killer. But what really piqued my master's interest was when I related Looney Liz Clawthorn's tale of the glowing hands.

"I know of the woman," Benelaius said thoughtfully. "She has the cataract, the veil over the eye that blurs and softens her sight. If she said she saw two waving hands . . ."

He left it for me to finish, and finish I did. "Lanterns," I said. "She saw two lanterns. Dovo must have had the one, but the other?"

"Someone Dovo was signaling to," said Lindavar, a catch of excitement in his voice. "That great mere we saw this morning would have been one of the few places in the Vast Swamp where signals could be given over long distances. Still," he said knowingly, "we saw no lantern by Dovo's body."

"But we did see lantern glass," said Benelaius.

"And that means—"

But I was not to know Benelaius's conclusion, for at that moment we were all startled by the flutter of wings at the window, which Benelaius had opened to disperse the heavy tobacco smoke. I gasped as I saw what sat on the sill.

It looked like a raven, but its body was half again as wide, and its wings equivalently longer. Its eyes glimmered an eerie greenish yellow in the candlelight, and they looked directly at Benelaius. The feet were more menacing than those of any normal bird, with three-inch talons at the end of pale, fleshy claws that looked like dead men's fingers. Around this creature's neck was a bag of thick leather knotted shut.

With a motion that made my breath catch in my throat, the weird bird hopped into the room and perched right on Benelaius's shoulder. It was a tribute to my master's calm that he moved not an iota at the bird's act. Then he turned his head toward the beak that could have pierced an eyeball with a single thrust, and smiled at the gleaming eyes.

"A good evening to you, Myrcrest," Benelaius said. "I hope that Vangerdahast, your master and my good friend, is well this night?"

The bird nodded its head slowly, and a guttural squawk escaped its thick throat. The sound sent chills through me like fingernails on slate. Even Lindavar winced.

But Benelaius was unshaken by the din. He raised his eyebrows and looked pleased. "I am glad to hear it," he said. Then he gestured toward the leather pouch. "And may I assume that inside is a message for me?"

Myrcrest nodded again, slowly and solemnly, like one of those toy birds that dips its beak in water over and over again.

"Then, with your kind permission . . ." Benelaius
lifted his hands and, with a series of deft, tiny strokes,
undid the pouch from around the great bird's neck. I
noticed in the light of the candles that Myrcrest's
feathers had no sheen to them at all. They gave back
no light but seemed rather to pull the light into them,
and kill it. I have never seen so flat and lusterless a
black. The thing must have noticed my attention, for
it fixed its beady eyes on me. I could not hold its gaze,
and quickly looked at Benelaius's hands.

He had freed the pouch and undid the string that
held it shut. From it he withdrew a heavy paper, folded many times, but when he unfolded it, the creases
vanished, and it was as smooth as though it had just
come off a press.

Benelaius read it, his composed and serious face
giving no hint as to the letter's matter. When he had
finished, he nodded once more at the fiendish bird on
his shoulder. "Pray tell Vangerdahast that his message has been received, and that its contents will be
obeyed. Fortune smile on him, and bid you speedily
home, good Myrcrest."

The bird nodded again, as graciously as a courtier.
Then it spread wide its wings, and I ducked at the
sudden movement, although the feathers were yards
away from my face. It leapt to the window, and then
through it, so that its blackness seemed sucked up by
the night. Its exit was so abrupt that at first I could
hardly believe it had been there at all.

But the paper that Benelaius held was the proof.
My master looked at Lindavar and me and said, "This
you should hear," and read:

Benelaius, my friend in wizardry—
Be it known by all men that Azoun, King of Cormyr,

*and I, Vangerdahast, Royal Magician and Chairman
Emeritus of the College of War Wizards of Cormyr, do
place in you our absolute trust concerning the appre-
hension of the murderer of Grodoveth, the envoy of the
King, and another victim.*

*When you have proven to your own satisfaction the
identity of this killer, whose act threatens the peace of
this good land, Captain Flim, or whoever may at that
time be commander of the local garrison of the King's
Purple Dragons, shall order his troops to immediately
put the murderer to death.*

Vangerdahast

"Well," said Benelaius, sitting back in his chair and
taking a deep puff upon his pipe. "That seems rather
final, does it not?"

27

"No arrest? No trial?" said Lindavar. "Why would the king order such a . . . a departure from the normal process of justice?"

"The king did *not* order it," said Benelaius. "Vangerdahast ordered it, and it is well within his power. It is altogether possible that King Azoun knows nothing of this order. Perhaps Vangerdahast felt it would be better for all concerned if he did not."

"But why?" I asked, echoing Lindavar. "I don't understand. I think that the king would want a trial of such a person, to make an example of what happens to those who would so openly flout his authority and kill his envoy."

"Unless," Benelaius said, "that envoy was a member by marriage of the royal family . . . and if the solution to the mystery cast aspersions on that envoy's honor. And, by extension, upon the honor of the king himself."

"Then Vangerdahast is trying to protect the king?" Lindavar asked.

"I think it likely," the old wizard said. "He loves his king more than he loves his magic, and Azoun is a good man and a good king. I doubt that he himself would make such an order as this that hints of self-protection." He removed his pipe from his teeth and tapped it on a metal bowl. The dottle dropped out, and he set the pipe next to it.

"But this command," he went on, "is contingent upon our finding the perpetrator in the first place, and that we have not yet done, though I fancy we have all the information we need. It is merely a matter of placing that information in the proper context and viewing it from the correct perspective." He smiled at me. "I suppose your Camber Fosrick would have done so far more quickly. Of course, he has the benefit of being a character in fiction, while we, unfortunately, are saddled with mundane reality. Still, we shall do our best."

"So what are your thoughts, sir?" I asked him, desperate to know what synthesis he had made of the disparate parts of this mystery.

"Still forming, I fear," Benelaius answered. "But even such infant musings would not have been possible without your diligence and hard work, my good Jasper. You have done superbly. But you must be very tired from all your labors, and the night has grown late. I suggest you retire to your bed. Kendra will be quite comfortable on the chaise for the night, and I wish to speak with Lindavar for a short time."

I had no choice but to obey. I would have loved to have been a fly on the wall, listening to their conversation, and when I was in my room, I tried to hear their talk, but since my quarters were at the opposite end of the cottage from Benelaius's study,

I heard only a low droning, out of which I could distinguish no separate words at all.

So I lay in the darkness and decided that I would not fall asleep until I had done what Benelaius had suggested was within the realm of possibility. I would determine who had killed Dovo and Grodoveth. I would come down with that information in the morning and dazzle them with my ratiocinative wizardry, and glory at the look of wonder and admiration in Benelaius's eyes.

And so I exercised my brain feverishly for all of three minutes, when exhaustion caught up with me and bashed me over the head.

But my concentration on the solution to the murders came with me into my dreams, and I remember waking up, convinced that I had the solution and the killer. In the darkness, I sleepily fumbled for the note pad and pencil with which I had taken notes for my master, and scribbled down several words that held the key to the mystery that had gained the attention of even the king himself. In the morning, even if I had forgotten the amazing revelations that came to me in my sleep, those words would still be there, and my sharing them with the world would bring me fame, honor, and riches. I fell back on the bed, smiling as sleep claimed me again.

I awoke at eight o'clock and had nearly finished my morning ablutions before I remembered that I had solved the murders in the middle of the night. And sure enough, as I had feared, I had no memory of the solution. So I dashed to the paper, snatched it up, and read:

Sunfirth-D made mess-fight-G-spilled? no tip?

Well, there it was then, all neatly wrapped up. I was sure that Benelaius would be happy to hear that Sunfirth, the five-foot two-inch, hundred-and-ten-pound barmaid, had beheaded both Dovo and Grodoveth with a single blow because Dovo, in his fight with Rolf, had made a mess for her to clean up, and because Grodoveth might have spilled something or left no gratuity for her services. On such a strong case, I had no doubt the Purple Dragons would execute her immediately and so end the threat to the kingdom.

In a pig's ear.

I decided that I would no longer trust my dreams, no matter how brilliant they might seem to a half-awake dullard like myself.

When I went downstairs to prepare breakfast, I got quite a surprise. There in the main room were Benelaius and Kendra, chatting and laughing like old friends. She was sitting up in the chaise, which she was sharing with a dozen contented cats, and my master was sitting next to her. They were both holding cups of tea, and so enthralled were they in their conversation that I had to clear my throat twice before they looked up.

"Ah, Jasper, good morning to you," said Benelaius. "I have to thank you for bringing such a delightful guest to our door last night. Kendra here has been to more places and seen more fascinating things than many a far older adventurer. She has added greatly to my store of information concerning the different species in areas of Faerûn to which I have never fared." Beaming, he turned back to the woman. "My dear, you make me wish to see those things firsthand."

"Why not?" said Kendra. "You're never too old for a new journey. And new experiences."

"Ah, but I may be too set in my ways to travel far. I have put down roots like an old mushroom here."

"But mushrooms have notoriously shallow roots,"

she said, and the coquettishness in her manner amazed me. Was this the woman who had been threatening men with disembowelment for looking twice at her? Maybe, I thought, she saw in Benelaius a nonthreatening father figure and thus felt free to flirt with him. But Benelaius? Flirting?

"You tempt me," he said, "but I fear I may strike out for no new horizons until the current crisis in Ghars is resolved. And to that end, Jasper," he said, turning to me, "I must send you into town again, as soon as you prepare a delicious and hearty breakfast to strengthen our temporary invalid here."

I needed no further cue. In the kitchen I put together a hot and healthy repast, and by the time I had it on the table, Lindavar had joined the party as well. Bags hung beneath his eyes, and I suspected that he and Benelaius had talked far into the night.

His appetite was good, however, and I never saw a woman eat as heartily as Kendra. Benelaius actually assisted her to the table, and although she favored her unwounded leg, my master assured her that only a small scar would be evidence of her battle with the hydra.

When the meal was finished, Benelaius handed me a long, thin leather courier's pouch and a small satchel. "Ride into Ghars," he said, "and deliver the letters in this pouch. The one addressed to Mayor Tobald and Captain Flim is the directive from Vangerdahast we received last night. Make sure they both read it, and leave it in Captain Flim's hands, since he is the one who will have to carry out the order . . . should the killer be taken. As far as making it general knowledge, tell them I advise against it, though I would be interested in seeing Barthelm Meadowbrock's reaction. Perhaps you can inform him privately.

"There is another envelope for Captain Flim alone, and there is also one for you, along with this satchel."

"Me?"

"Yes. Open and read the letter when you are ready to return here. At that time you will understand the need for what is in the satchel. Oh, and I almost forgot . . ." He reached into his robe and, smiling wryly, took out a bottle of small white pills. "Mayor Tobald's gout medication. Please give this to him in private. I don't want anyone to tell Doctor Braum that I'm treating his patient. Braum's a good man, though only a fair doctor, and I don't wish to offend him."

Benelaius and Lindavar came out to bid me farewell, while Kendra returned to the comfort of her chaise and the cats, who had taken quite a liking to her. As I turned Jenkus and prepared to ride away, Benelaius held up a chubby hand. "One thing yet, Jasper. I suggest you drink ale today." And he placed into my hand several coins to make such a request possible.

I thought I had misheard him and asked to him to repeat what he had said.

"Ale today, Jasper. If you are thirsty, drink only ale. Don't ask why. Just humor an old man."

Though it was one of my master's more eccentric requests, I nodded acceptance and rode toward Ghars, wondering if the great man's mental faculties had been temporarily dulled by a Mirtul-Eleint infatuation with Kendra, or by a constant and deep concentration on the solution to the murders.

But in retrospect, I thought his command an easy and even fun one to obey. Rare is the master who tells his man, "Go and drink ale, my boy!" So I decided to consider myself lucky, and rode happily toward Ghars.

28

I heard the humming in the town while I was still a quarter mile south. If yesterday's flurry of preparation had been busy, then today's was a cyclone of activity. Although supposedly everything had been long prepared, there were apparently half a hundred unexpected occurrences that had to be taken care of.

I found Captain Flim on his horse in the town square. Behind him were a dozen Purple Dragons watching the scene, ready, no doubt, to lay waste to any Zhentarim spy bold enough to announce his intentions. In truth, they were there to preserve order, although such a task at that time was well nigh impossible.

I told Captain Flim that Benelaius had had a communication from Suzail that both he and Tobald should be aware of. He nodded brusquely and led the way to the Sheaf of Wheat, where Tobald and Barthelm were overseeing the final arrangements for the arrival of the guild leaders. The captain and I dismounted, and he beckoned Tobald over. When Flim beckoned, even the mayor reacted quickly, albeit with a hasty limp. His gout, I could see, had worsened.

We miraculously found a quiet room in the inn, and I closed the door behind us as we entered. Then I read Vangerdahast's directive to them, and showed them the missive itself.

"Excellent!" Tobald said. "As much as I dislike violence, only such an extreme act can restore honor to our town. Captain Flim, are you ready to follow these orders?"

Flim's expression didn't change a jot. "I am. What comes from Vangerdahast is as good as from the king himself. A Purple Dragon follows his king's orders, and I've not a man in the garrison who wouldn't cut down his own mother if Benelaius would say she was the murderer."

"Oh, my," Tobald said, shaking his head. "Let's hope it doesn't come to that."

"I doubt it," I said lightly. "I don't think any of the Dragons' mothers are under suspicion. By the by, Captain, Benelaius wanted you to take possession of that letter, and this is also for you from my master." I handed him the letter, and he looked at his name on it.

"Shall I read it now?" he asked, as though it made no difference to him, now or later.

I shrugged, and he broke the seal and read. His face underwent no change. "Tell Benelaius I'll do as he asks," Captain Flim said, and walked out the door, leaving me alone with Tobald.

"Lord Mayor," I said, "before you return to your preparations, I have something for you from my master as well," and I handed him the bottle of pills.

He beamed in relief. "Thank the gods," he said, and

opened the top and swallowed one down without water, making a face as he did so. "And thank your master," he said. "I've been so anxious for these."

Then he was off again into the fray. I think I worked less hard as a slop boy.

Finding myself alone in the small meeting room at the Sheaf of Wheat, I decided to indulge myself by merely sitting and luxuriating in sloth at the place where I used to work so diligently and for such low pay. Sitting in one of the comfy chairs near the dead fireplace, I took out Benelaius's letter and opened it.

It was brief, and instructed me to remain in Ghars and place myself at the service of Captain Flim, who would be leading a party to Benelaius's cottage late that evening. I should return home then. It told me to also attend the welcoming fete to be held at the Sheaf of Wheat that evening, and that Captain Flim would see to it that I was admitted. Inside the satchel were my best dress clothes. The letter ended with the words, "Watch everyone."

Quite a trick, I thought, what with the hundreds milling in the streets and the dozens who were to come that day. But I would do my best. Before putting myself at Captain Flim's service, however, I had one more thing to do.

I found Barthelm Meadowbrock at a long table outside the Sheaf of Wheat. He was going through large sacks of woven silver mesh that were to be given to each attendee. They were filled with examples of the wares of Ghars, both food and crafts, and Barthelm peered into each one as though he were expecting a serpent to slither out of it.

He looked up when I hailed him, and frowned at me. "What d'you want?" he barked, turning his attention to another bag.

"Just to bring you relief, good sir," quoth I. "I know

how anxious you are that the killer of Dovo and
Grodoveth be found and punished." He frowned even
more deeply at the mention of the two names. "So
you will be pleased to know that an order has come
from Suzail commanding that the killer, once discovered, is to be immediately executed by the Purple
Dragons."

He stopped looking through bags for a moment,
stared off into the distance thoughtfully, then turned
with a jerk to me. "Well, *that* ought to discourage this
kind of thing from happening again. Bloody inconve-
nient, these murders, what with the guild council
coming and all . . ." He continued to mutter as he
turned his attention back to the sacks.

I wondered if that was the reaction Benelaius had
expected. Did my master suspect Barthelm of being
the killer? If so, then the merchant should have
grasped his neck at the news and muttered, "Urk," or
something of the sort. But then, murderers would be
more skilled at hiding their feelings. At least *successful* murderers would. That was what made it so hard
to catch them, wasn't it?

I decided to follow Benelaius's orders and presented myself to Captain Flim for his further service, but
he just shook his head. "There's nothing I'll need you
for until after the fete tonight. I'll see to it that you can
get in. In the meantime, you're on your own. Do what
you like."

So I did. I hung around the square, watching others work, which was quite a novelty. At noon, I went
into the Bold Bard and had a bowl of soup and an ale,
since Benelaius had told me to drink it exclusively,
and then I went out and watched the busy bees some
more.

The council of the Merchants' Guild began to
arrive by midafternoon, and that was fun to watch.

Nearly all were rotund (wealth meant good eating, I saw), and all were accompanied by retinues of servants and hangers-on. The merchants of Ghars fell all over themselves in their desire to properly greet the nabobs, and I swear that I saw old Menchuk, the dry-goods seller, shovel up piles of horse droppings left by one leader's entourage so that the smell would not offend the next leader to arrive. I had to laugh, for he moved so quickly that one would have thought he was shoveling up diamonds.

Some of the councilmen were sent to the Sheaf of Wheat, and others to the Silver Scythe, but first, all were presented by Mayella Meadowbrock with the ceremonial food and drink of welcome, which consisted of a piece of fresh elven bread arrived that morning from the Isle of Evermeet, and a silver goblet of fresh water. After their brief repast, Mayella gave each of them their silver sack of goodies while Barthelm spoke words of welcome.

From the libidinous looks that some of the leaders gave the girl, I felt sure they would have rather been presented with the beauteous Mayella herself. But none of them made any overt propositions in that regard, so the protective Barthelm was able to keep his temper under control.

By late afternoon, the last of the councilmen and his party had arrived. They had all retired to their rooms at either the Sheaf of Wheat or the Silver Scythe for a washup and a change of clothes, and I did likewise, putting on the garments that Benelaius had packed for me.

At seven o'clock, everyone gathered in the great room of the Sheaf of Wheat. Since the Silver Scythe would host the meeting the next day, the Sheaf of Wheat would play host to the grand reception.

Silver medallions that had been given to the guests

upon their arrival were their entry into the reception. Captain Flim had gotten one for me through Mayor Tobald. Beneath the medallion was suspended a piece of parchment with one's name and home city on it, along with one's position, such as Council President or Council Member. Mine stated Council Special Guest, and I hoped I would be allowed to keep the medallion later, since the silver in it weighed as much as five falcons.

Lukas Spoondrift himself was guarding the door, graciously admitting only those with the proper credential pinned to their chests. When my ex-boss saw me, he half-smiled, half-sneered, and I could see that he was anxious to give this supposed gate crasher the boot. "And where do you think you're going, slop boy?" he said in a rather inhospitable tone.

"Not slop boy," I corrected him as I tapped my medallion meaningfully. "Special guest of the Cormyrean Merchant's Guild council. And one who expects gracious hospitality. I hope, Spoondrift, for your sake, that everything surpasses the Sheaf of Wheat's usual fare. I intend to savor every dish tonight, looking for your old tricks of putting mutton in the lamb stew, and adding horsemeat to the beef dishes. I was not totally blind during my tenure with you, you know. And any such corner cutting for the sake of economy will be reported to the council, of whom I am a"—I glanced down meaningfully at my title—"special guest."

His face worked for a long time, but he finally succeeded in hiding his hatred of me and smiled the most appalling, insincere grimace I have ever seen. But at least it was an attempt at sincerity, and there was nothing of the demeaning sneer in it, so I knew I had him by the scruff. "I beg your pardon . . . sir," he said, every word coming out like a pulled tooth.

Chet Williamson

"Welcome to this . . . humble inn, and if I may be of any assistance, you have but to ask."

Then he bowed, and it was all I could do not to laugh. Demeaning himself did not come easily to Spoondrift. I bowed in return, and passed by him into the grand reception.

29

Barthelm Meadowbrock had done a good job of pushing Spoondrift to put his best foot forward. There were several buffet tables, and other smaller tables for the councilmen to sit at, if they didn't wish to stand and eat, as most of them were doing. The dishes were first rate, and I sampled nearly everything. No horsemeat in this stag sausage, though I thought I did detect a bit of mutton in the lamb stew.

Still, everything was cooked so well and presented so elegantly that I thought it expedient to overlook the mutton. The Sheaf of Wheat's staff did much of the serving, but many of the town lovelies helped as well, including the dazzling Mayella Meadowbrock, who was dishing out an oyster and wild rice concoction that seemed to be the most delicious dish available, if the long line was any indication. I noticed a few councilmen gobbling down the food as though they hadn't eaten in weeks, just so they could get back in line and face the radiant Mayella once again.

I must confess to two helpings myself, even though I detest oysters.

At one point I stood in line next to Mayor Tobald, who was beaming with good health and, I assumed, several mugs of Suzale or Elminster's Choice. "A grand evening, Jasper," he said, clapping me on the shoulder. "A grand evening." And I had to confess it was.

Some of the councilmen had brought their wives along. Most were old, fat and snobbish sorts, but a few were young and extremely attractive. Surprisingly, these were usually with the oldest and most physically repellent men, and I was cynical enough to note that if money cannot buy love, it can purchase a decent enough simulacrum of the same.

But for most of the party, it was boy's night out. They ate and laughed and drank and told amazingly ribald stories for such pillars of the Cormyrean community. But their long travels wore them down early, and by ten o'clock, the official closing time of the reception, most had wandered back to their rooms, though some of the hardier ones congregated at the bars of the Sheaf of Wheat or the Silver Scythe, depending on which inn they were staying at. Some even went across town to the Bold Bard for their nightcap.

I heard Barthelm Meadowbrock tell Mayella that he was going to be joining some of the councilmen over at Shortshanks's tavern, but that was before Captain Flim came up to him and spoke quietly. I couldn't hear what he said, but I certainly heard Barthelm's reaction.

"What! Flim, you must be mad! You can't expect me to leave now and go out to . . . to that old wizard's! I have business to conduct, contacts to make. . . ."

Since this conversation no doubt concerned my

master, I moved in closer and heard Captain Flim's reply. "Begging your pardon, sir, but the wizard Benelaius's orders are to be obeyed by me as if they came from King Azoun himself, and if Benelaius says to bring you and your daughter to his house tonight, so it shall be."

"It bloody well shall *not*!" growled Barthelm. "I am the host of this gathering, and—"

"And the host shall find himself taken in chains to Benelaius's if he will not go willingly," said Flim. "Hardly the image you wish to project to your fellow merchants." Oh, yes, Captain Flim could be quite persuasive when he had to be.

"Are you threatening me?" Barthelm said.

"I am telling you, sir, that I will obey my orders and bring you to Benelaius's house any way I must."

Barthelm fumed for a few minutes, then nodded his head briskly. "Very well. Give me a minute to say my farewells and have the coach brought round."

"Take your time," said Captain Flim. "I have a few more citizens to gather. Benelaius wants us there by midnight."

"Midnight," grumbled Barthelm. "Oh, I'll be so alert for the meeting tomorrow. . . ."

Captain Flim buttonholed Mayor Tobald then, who seemed just about ready to head off for more drinking with some convivial merchants. His ruddy face sobered quickly, and he nodded, looking concerned, I thought, that no news of this murderous scandal reach the ears of the councilmen.

"I have four more people to gather," Flim told me after his talk with Tobald. "Rolf and Shortshanks will be at the Bold Bard, and I've already sent my men to the houses of Marmwitz and Khlerat."

Phelos Marmwitz and old Khlerat? There was a pair. The ancient librarian and the retired dabbler in public works. Maybe it was a geriatric conspiracy.

"Have your horse ready outside the Bold Bard in twenty minutes," Captain Flim concluded. "We'll ride out to Benelaius's together."

"Will you be taking any Purple Dragons along?" I asked.

"A dozen good men," Captain Flim said, and walked out the door.

A dozen men. That meant that something was going to happen at Benelaius's, sure enough, and I recalled the thrilling scenes in the Camber Fosrick tales where Fosrick gathered together all the suspects, confronted them with the evidence, and identified the killer. Now Benelaius was going to create the same situation, but in reality. As much as he frowned on the Fosrick mysteries, I could not help but think that he had read them—and learned from them too.

I had Jenkus ready to go within minutes, and waited impatiently as the parties gathered. Barthelm and Mayella Meadowbrock were already there, Barthelm looking annoyed, Mayella looking as though she were willing to accept whatever life and her daddy threw at her. Tobald came riding up on his strong if none too fast mare, and shortly after, four soldiers rode up surrounding Rolf, who appeared nothing short of livid. I think he might have broken through them and run for it, but for the fact that they had him mounted on a very old, very tired horse.

Then a commotion broke out down the street in the person of one man—or dwarf. Shortshanks was riding a small mount between Captain Flim and one of his Purple Dragons, and I've seldom heard a dwarf so mad. "Tak' me away from my tavern on the best night of all the years I've been here, will ya! I'll have yer stripes fer this, Flim, I *will*! Of all the idiotic things I've seen the military do, this takes the cake, deprivin' a dwarf of his livelihood . . . if I were a human, you'd not be doin' this to me, I wager!"

"You're wrong, dwarf," said Captain Flim. "I'm doing the same thing to the most powerful man in town, so shut your little yap before I do something I'll be sorry for."

"Little! He called me little! Did ye hear that?"

"Yes," said Flim wearily. "They all heard it, just as they hear me tell you now that if you don't pipe down, you're liable to be even littler—by a head." Shortshanks glowered but said nothing. "Besides," Captain Flim continued, "your worst troublemaker's already with us here, and not back at your tavern, so you've naught to fear. Ah . . . here's the last of our party."

Two more dragons came riding up on either side of a small carriage. Old Khlerat was driving the two horses, and Marmwitz was sitting next to him.

"Let's be getting out to Benelaius's then," said Captain Flim, and he spurred his horse and our caravan started off. The Dragons positioned themselves ahead and behind, left and right, to prevent any of the involuntary travelers from leaving the party, or so I assumed.

There was much to think about as we rode south toward Benelaius's cottage and the Vast Swamp. Captain Flim, Tobald, and the Dragons were there in their official capacity, but I wondered greatly about the others.

Barthelm might have had a motive for both slayings in fatherly protection. And Rolf could have slain both Dovo and Grodoveth out of jealousy. Shortshanks had little to gain from either death, unless, of course, Dovo had been driving customers away from the Swamp Rat at his behest and was threatening to talk about it. The dwarf could even have followed Grodoveth to the tomb. But then, so could anyone else.

Kendra was already at Benelaius's and I wondered if my master would have had the Dragons take her there if she were not. I doubted she would have gone voluntarily, and thought it fortunate, if she was a suspect, that she had suffered her wound the night before.

As for the presence of Marmwitz and Khlerat, I was at a loss. Two harmless old men, as far as I was concerned. But I would learn in my life that what appeared harmless might not necessarily be so.

30

It seemed like a funeral procession going through the night. We didn't speak or laugh or whisper. We rode, and the only sounds were the horses' hooves striking the road, the creak of the leather saddles, and the rattle of the carriage's wheels and boards.

In the strong company of a dozen Purple Dragons, I felt no fear as we passed the spot where I had seen the "ghost" and found its body the next day. In fact, I strained my eyes looking into that murky darkness at the swamp's edge, just daring a ghost or hydra or zombie to appear. I was tense and edgy, and felt as though I wanted to confront something. But I saw nothing except the darkness of the night and the edge of the swamp, a deeper blackness against the black.

The Swamp Rat was nearly deserted, but those who were there came out and watched us ride past. I saw old Farmer Bortas with his two cronies, Rob and Will, and he waved at me. Rob and Will didn't wave. I guess they still didn't cotton to me.

"Say there, young feller," Farmer Bortas called. "What's all this great parade, eh?"

"We're going to my master's house. Benelaius."

"Aye? I didn't fancy him as the partyin' type. Well, you all have yourselves a good time now, lad, and don't drink too much, eh?"

The others in our party turned a sullen look on the farmer, and he lost his smile. He turned to Rob and Will, and I heard him say softly, "Now that's a party I wouldn't give half a copper to go to. What are they cellybratin', somebody's hexycution?"

He didn't know how right he was. We rode on, toward Benelaius and the truth.

The final half mile seemed the longest. All the horses became nervous as we neared the body of the hydra, which had been dragged off the road and left to rot. You could smell it already, and I made a mental note to come out and try to burn it, for if the wind blew from the west, the stench of its rotting would reach the cottage and plague it for weeks. Far better to endure the sharper but far briefer smell of its burning.

But perhaps there wouldn't be as much to burn as I had thought. As we rode by the hydra's bulky corpse, we heard the scuttling of dozens of predators who had been feasting through the night on its carcass, the same way, I thought grimly, the councilmen had been wolfing down their treats in Ghars. The dead creature's severed heads were probably already gone, dragged off into the swamp for a more leisurely meal. I shuddered and looked back at the road ahead.

As we rounded the final bend, I saw that all the lights were burning at the cottage, including the large one on the post near the road. There were lights in back of the house as well, as though the braziers that ringed the piazza were all burning. The light shone weakly upon the Vast Swamp itself, and it had never looked closer to the house than on this night. It seemed a huge lump of malevolent life that needed only to hump up just a bit higher to crush the cottage and destroy all the light in and around it forever.

Or maybe that was just my imagination.

I was feeling a little jumpy, and more than ready to hear what Benelaius was going to say. You don't pull a dozen Purple Dragons, their captain, and a wagon load of important or easily irritable townspeople out to the swamp in the middle of the night unless you've got something big to tell them.

Lindavar emerged from the front door as our caravan came lumbering up, and bowed with more grace than I had previously seen in him. "Greetings," he said.

Barthelm Meadowbrock was in no mood for niceties. "What's the meaning of this? Why has that madman of a wizard had us all brought out here at sword point?"

"Our swords, sir," said Captain Flim with a touch of pique, "are all sheathed."

Lindavar held up a calming hand to quiet any further disputes. "Benelaius is waiting for us on the piazza in the back of the house. There he will explain why your presences have been required."

Two of the twelve soldiers stayed with the horses, and I allowed them to watch Jenkus as well. I could rub him down later. Lindavar led us into the house, the rest of the soldiers flanking all of us, with me and Mayor Tobald bringing up the rear.

The cats, even though unused to such hordes of company, parted like the waters of an enchanted sea as we passed through them. Mayella murmured, "Pretty kitties," and leaned to pat a few, who responded with deeply appreciative purrs.

But over their mellow rumbling, I heard the louder sound of one of the feline congregation hissing, but when I turned to look, I saw only Mayor Tobald, his face set in a grimace. He smiled quickly, as if to show nothing was wrong, and we continued on through the main room and Benelaius's study, and out the doors to the piazza in the rear of the dwelling.

There Benelaius sat in a large chair next to Kendra, who still occupied the chaise, which I assumed Lindavar had moved outside. There were also nine wooden chairs that I had never seen used before in the cottage. They were designed to stack one atop the other, and had always been stored in a closet. Four braziers sat on the piazza rail, providing enough light for all of us to see one another. Two of our cats sat beside each brazier, making quite a picturesque arrangement.

Benelaius rose to his feet and smiled at the assembled multitudes. "Pray forgive me for keeping all of you from your well-deserved rest," he said, "or your further joyous celebrations at hosting such a distinguished gathering as the Grand Council of the Cormyrean Merchants' Guild. I assure you that each of your presences was required here tonight. All will be explained in a short while, but what most of you probably already suspect is true. It does indeed have to do with the murders that have caused such pain in Ghars."

"Then tell us what you want to tell us, Benelaius," said Barthelm, "and let us go home!"

"Patience, please, my dear Barthelm. This is not something that can be done in haste. It may take a bit of time to sort out all the pieces and put them together again." He looked at Captain Flim, who was standing stolidly by, his hand on his sword hilt. "I don't think we'll need your soldiers just yet, Captain Flim."

"Just the same, sir, I'd rather have them here and not need them than need them and not have them."

"A wise answer, Captain," said Benelaius, "and I bow to your greater military experience. Position your men as you see fit. Now," he said, sitting back down, "I would ask all of you—except the soldiers on duty, of course—to please take a seat. Yes, that's fine. Jasper, on my right. Lord Mayor, on my left if you will." I sat where I was told, while Tobald made his way, with a slight limp, to Benelaius's left. The others sat as well. "Good, very good. Everyone comfortable? Excellent.

"As you may or may not know, I have been appointed, first at the request of Mayor Tobald, and then in a more official manner by Vangerdahast, Royal Wizard to King Azoun, to study the recent murders in the Vast Swamp and see if I could solve the mystery of who the killer was. I have been fortunate in having the aid of two excellent helpers—Jasper, who has done much of my legwork, occasionally at the risk of his life and limb, and Lindavar, the newest member of the College of War Wizards. Jasper has gathered an immense and enlightening wealth of information, and Lindavar has helped me beyond words to take that information and blend it into a theory . . . nay, more than a theory. An absolute proof as to who killed Dovo and Grodoveth."

"You've found the killer?" Barthelm said, nearly starting from his chair.

"I . . . we have," said Benelaius, acknowledging Lindavar. "And in this case, such definite proof is needed, for orders have come from Suzail that the killer, once his identity is exposed, is to be immediately executed by the military authority." The wizard gestured toward the stolid but watchful Purple Dragons standing to one side of the piazza. "And that is why they are here this night."

"You mean to say," said Shortshanks, his legs dangling from his chair, "that these soldiers are gonna do for the killer right here?"

"I am not sure," answered Benelaius. "Captain Flim, what will be the procedure?"

"Hanging," Captain Flim said. "From the nearest tree."

"Ah-hah," said Benelaius mildly. "And there will be no opportunity to plead for innocence, I take it?"

"None."

"That is why," Benelaius said in the same pedantic tone he sometimes used when tutoring me, "there must be no mistake. And when you have heard our evidence and conclusions, I think that none of us—not even the murderer—will doubt that we are correct in our accusation.

"I must give the lion's share of credit, however, to Lindavar. It was he who came up with most of our conclusions, and I think that once you hear them, you will agree that he has done a splendid job of reasoning."

"Are we gonna find out tonight?" Rolf asked, "or are you gonna talk us all to death?"

Benelaius only smiled benevolently. "I don't blame you for your impatience, young man. But when we are dealing with a person's very life, we cannot afford to be rushed and slipshod. I would like Lindavar to explain our deductions, and perhaps you will find his discourse a bit less rambling than my own."

At that, Benelaius nodded to the younger wizard,

who stood up, nervously cleared his throat, and looked at the assemblage. Then he began to talk, very softly, so that even I, who have good ears, could not make out all the words.

"Speak up!" said Barthelm. "Can't hear a thing!"

Lindavar cleared his throat again and bowed apologetically. When he next spoke, his tone wasn't commanding, but at least I could hear him. "Most of you are here," he said, "because you have been considered as possible suspects in the murders of Dovo and Grodoveth."

"What!" Rolf said, leaping to his feet. "I had nothin' to do with that weasel gettin' himself killed, nor that old one either! And the man who says I do—"

Rolf broke off quickly as two of the Purple Dragons slammed him back into his seat and held him there. "Another outburst like that, young fellow," Captain Flim said, "and you'll be in chains with a gag around your head. In fact, I might just hang you on general principles. Now hush yourself."

Rolf glowered at the captain but said nothing more. I heard his angry breath hissing in and out like a swarm of bees.

"As . . . I was saying," Lindavar went on, "suspicion has fallen on many of you. The young lady here, our involuntary guest"—he glanced at Kendra, who smiled coldly, petting one of the three cats that had made her lap their home—"was . . . spoken to by both Dovo and the king's envoy in a manner not altogether . . . gentlemanly."

"You mean they came on to me like pigs," Kendra said dryly.

"In a word," Lindavar said, still not looking in her direction. "Jasper informed us of all that was said by all the parties that night. And you *are* rather quick with a sword."

"The killings were done with an axe," Kendra reminded us.

"And I suppose you've never seen one of those before," put in Captain Flim, who still eyed Kendra suspiciously.

"And me?" Barthelm said. "Why am *I* considered a suspect? I, a member of the Merchants' Guild Grand Council!"

"Because any man can be an angry and protective father," Benelaius said, calming the waters. "Both victims offered some insult to your daughter, Mayella, as well as Kendra. But whereas Kendra is skilled at fending off such clumsy advances, your daughter, good Barthelm, is not. It would not be beyond imagining that you should try to defend her honor, as a good father would be expected to do."

"Or a sincere suitor," said Lindavar to Rolf, "which explains your presence here tonight, young man. You have also a hot temper, which you have demonstrated for us."

"Fine, all right then," Rolf spat out. "You think I did it? Take me out and hang me then—I'd die a dozen deaths to defend Mayella's honor!"

"That may or may not be necessary," Benelaius said. "Proceed, Lindavar."

"What about me?" Shortshanks interrupted. "Why'm *I* here? I had naught to do with that girl!"

"No," said Lindavar. "But you did benefit from Dovo's haunting of the swamp. It kept folk away from the Swamp Rat and brought them to the Bold Bard instead. And not to make any prejudicial statement, but I don't think a dwarf's been born that doesn't lust after hidden treasure, the kind found in Fastred's tomb. Also, an axe was used, and every dwarf warrior's weapon of choice is an axe."

"Well, I'm not a warrior, am I, Mister War Wizard

Smarty-Pants? I'm a barkeep, in case you haven't noticed. Come down out of your ivory tower and drop by, and I'll give ye an ale, if you're man enough to handle it."

"And what was given to Dovo, I wonder," said Lindavar, starting to get into it now, "to frighten people away from the swamp? Jasper, tell Mr. Shortshanks what you found in the men's necessary room of his establishment."

"I found Dovo's cloak and hat," I said.

"Which would lead someone of a suspicious nature to think he used the Bold Bard as a base of operations." Lindavar held up a hand to cut off Shortshanks's expected reaction. "But we'll come back to that later."

"What about those two?" said Barthelm, pointing to Khlerat and Marmwitz, both of whom looked extremely nervous. "Did they do it too? Or were we all in it together?" he finished scornfully.

"Their presence here will be explained shortly," said Lindavar. "Now let us turn from suspicions to evidence. Of all the mystifying things about these murders, one of the most baffling was not the presence of a certain piece of evidence, but its absence. Or at least the absence of most of it.

"What were the chances that Dovo—or anyone for that matter—would go into the Vast Swamp at night without a lantern? Granted, the areas near the edges of the swamp are less dangerous than those farther in. But still, it would be foolhardy to go at night without a light. There are patches of quicksand, clinging mire, bottomless pools, hundreds of natural dangers to ensnare the unwary.

"Yet when Dovo's body was found, no extinguished or burned-out lantern was found near him, only a few pieces of curved glass from a broken lantern, probably his own. But the killer did not leave the lantern with the body. Instead he took it. Why?

"The absence of that lantern is the missing piece that enables the others to fall into place. The lantern was taken because the killer didn't want us to know that Dovo had a lantern in the first place. That meant that he must have been using that lantern for something other than light. And the one who told us what that purpose was, was Elizabeth Clawthorn."

"Looney Liz?" said Rolf. "Who'd believe anything she said?"

"Jasper would. And so would I. Jasper, tell us what Mrs. Clawthorn saw."

"She followed Dovo into the swamp," I said, "to that large open area near where Darvik found Grodoveth's body and Fastred's tomb. She saw Dovo signaling with his lantern to someone across the mere. And she saw someone signal back."

"So the lantern was used for signals," Lindavar said. "Signals to someone on the other side of the Vast Swamp. Or someone who came from there through the swamp. And what lies southeast of the swamp?"

"Sembia," said Mayor Tobald. "You mean he was signaling to someone in Sembia?" The mayor thought for a moment. "There are a good number of Zhentarim agents in that country, are there not, Captain Flim?"

But Flim didn't have a chance to answer, for Lindavar spoke instantly. "There are indeed, Lord Mayor, and other villains besides. More than just Zhentarim agents have been captured near here recently."

"The Iron Throne," muttered Captain Flim.

"Precisely," said Lindavar. "The Iron Throne."

"Wait a minute," Rolf said. "You telling me a bunch of merchants killed Dovo and the envoy?"

"More than just a . . . bunch of merchants, lad," Benelaius said. "They are a secret and dangerous organization, headed by parties unknown but thought to have its primary backers in the land of Sembia." Benelaius patted Grimalkin on his lap and nodded. "Sembia's merchants are ruthless in their business dealings."

"Like the old saying," Lindavar added, " 'When you look into a Sembian's eyes, you can see coins being counted in his mind.' Sembia was built on trade, so it lives and dies by it. And when it comes to matters of life and death, people are not always scrupulous. Elduth Yarmmaster, the Overmaster of Sembia, has been a voice of reason in the past, but he grows old and may not live out his term. In the meantime, the Iron Throne has done much that the elected government would not dare to do, even if its leaders were able to overcome Elduth's sage council."

"Like what then?" asked Shortshanks.

"Assassinating their competitors, extortion, selling illegal substances, trading weapons to inhuman tribes . . . the list goes on and on. The difficulty is that the Iron Throne's backers are unknown. They work through lower-level thugs for the most part. But still, the behavior of their agents has become so heinous that King Azoun banned the Iron Throne from acting within Cormyr for a year. Since the balance of trade between Cormyr and other kingdoms greatly affects the manipulations of the Iron Throne and of Sembian trade, it became imperative that the Iron Throne seek out that information, but with its agents arrested as soon as they set foot into Cormyr, this became more and more difficult.

"So if the Iron Throne could not legitimately enter

our country and gather trade and production information, it would have to acquire that knowledge by stealth."

"Wait a minute now," said Shortshanks impatiently. "Are you sayin' that all this killin' was just to tell a gaggle of merchants how much oats and barley was gettin' grown and comin' in and out of the country?"

"That's exactly what I'm saying," Lindavar answered, "though how you put it is too simplistic. The information needed probably covered crop output, trade routes, what was to be exported, and what would be transported to different parts of Cormyr. Since the area around Ghars is basically agrarian, that was the intelligence that would be conveyed to the Iron Throne in Sembia.

"In more industrial sections of the kingdom, and in areas that rely on crafts, I have no doubt that Iron Throne agents are telling their masters how many swords and pots and saddles and boots are being made and where they are being sent. It sounds like a stream of mundane information, but it can be the lifeblood of a country that depends on trade for its livelihood. A country like Sembia, and an organization like the Iron Throne."

"So when Dovo was signaling with this lantern that the killer had taken away," said Captain Flim, as if getting it straight in his mind, "he was giving this information to the Iron Throne?" Lindavar nodded. "But how do you know that? And what was all the ghost claptrap for?"

"We'll come to how we know it was the Iron Throne in a moment," said Lindavar. "But the ghost was simply for cover. If Dovo had been seen walking off the swamp road with a lantern, questions would have been asked. What was he doing walking into the swamp at night? So the best strategy, and one that

worked, was for him to dress up as the ghost of
Fastred, an apparition that would make nearly everyone run the other way in fright. If Dovo heard horses' hooves, or someone walking along the road who
might see him, he went into the ghost routine and
scared them away, then moved into the swamp and
did . . . what he was supposed to do."

"Dovo?" Rolf said in disbelief. "Look, I know you're
a War Wizard and all that, but you expect us to
believe that somebody as dumb as Dovo was could
even get all this information you're talking about, let
alone come up with this ghost idea? He scarcely had
the brains to hammer on a horseshoe!"

"All he had to do was learn the code," Lindavar
said. "He might not have even realized what he was
doing. Perhaps he was told that he was transmitting
information to smugglers, or someone less repre-
hensible than the Iron Throne. Whatever he was told,
he was also told all the information the Iron Throne
needed."

"Told by whom?" Barthelm demanded. "What
Cormyrean would betray his king and country?"

"And the local merchants, eh?" Shortshanks said
with a sneer.

"The information was derived from someone who
had easy access to it, someone whose official capacity not only allowed him but *required* him to know
these things and report them to the local lord, Sarp
Redbeard, in Wheloon. This person was a repository
of export and trade information from Thunderstone
to the Way of the Manticore, in all the lands between
the Wyvernwater and the Vast Swamp. And it was
from him that the information came, the same information that Dovo then gave the agents of the Iron
Throne across the Vast Swamp."

"Grodoveth . . ." Mayor Tobald said softly.

"Grodoveth was a spy in the employ of the Iron Throne." And he put his head in his hands and shuddered, and I felt great pity come upon me for this man whose friend had betrayed his country.

"Grodoveth," he moaned once again.

31

The room was quiet for a moment, as all eyes were on the mayor and his sorrow. But then Lindavar spoke again. "No. Not Grodoveth. You need have no worry on that account, Lord Mayor. Grodoveth was but an innocent conduit of that information, telling what he had seen and what he knew without hesitation to someone he had no reason to distrust.

"That Grodoveth was the source is apparent from a look at the dates. The ghostly appearances, and thus the secret signals, always occurred just after Grodoveth visited Ghars. There was one exception when no ghost was seen, and the reasonable conclusion to draw is simply that no one saw Dovo from the road that particular night.

"So the intelligence went from Grodoveth to the Iron Throne agent to Dovo. It was that agent who recruited Dovo into his plans, perhaps winning him over with a romantic story of smugglers, or even Cormyrean agents. Along with the exciting risk was the fun of terrorizing everyone in the town, and, of course, money.

"But Dovo made a mistake. He became cocky, though I suspect he already was. When he approached Kendra, he told her that there was more to him than she might think—'much more.' When his secret employer overheard this comment, he panicked, and with good reason. It was only a short step from Dovo telling a paramour that he was the ghost to having the entire story come out, including the agent's participation. He knew he had to silence Dovo before he said too much, and the most efficient way to do that was to terminate his ghostly career by killing him.

"He met him at the swamp, made some excuse to examine his axe, and beheaded him, making it look like the act of a vengeful ghost who would bear no mockery. Grodoveth already had an interest in local legends, is that not so, Mr. Marmwitz?"

"Oh, yes," Marmwitz said, nodding frantically, recognizing that this was his shining moment. "He was always looking over the books on local folklore, particularly anything to do with the Vast Swamp."

"And it was impossible that he could have done all that reading without coming across the legend of Fastred, was it not?"

"Oh, no," said Marmwitz, still bobbing like a cork in a squall. "I mean, yes . . . I mean, I'm certain he would have come across Fastred, oh my, yes."

"And coming across stories of the old warrior-brigand, he might have suspected, as did most of us, that Dovo's death was due, not to a ghost, but to foul play, and, as it turned out, from the foulest motives. His investigations into the legend of Fastred were so deep that he figured out the riddle that has puzzled many people for years—the location of Fastred's tomb. What better place, he thought, for the hiding place of the murderer. And if, on the other hand, the murderer was not even cognizant of the hidden tomb, what a treat its discovery would be for the historians of Cormyr.

"And he found it. But he also found the killer. Or the killer found him. He struck quickly, so that Grodoveth did not even have a chance to defend himself. To the superstitious, it would have looked like one more act of revenge from beyond the grave, this time for entering Fastred's tomb and disturbing his rest. The only thing is, if that were the case, Fastred's treasure would still have been there. But it was gone, taken by the killer, either then or long before, if he had indeed discovered the location of the tomb before Grodoveth had.

"But the killer made one mistake, one foolish error of the type that has tripped up far more clever criminals than he. He left something behind him—a clue, which Jasper was alert enough to find. Something that pointed the finger of suspicion at him enough for us to investigate further.

"We surreptitiously searched his personal belongings and found a certain vial. When we analyzed the contents of that vial, we found that it was poison. Blackweed, extremely potent but slow acting. Once it had been ingested by the victim, there would be no sign of its presence until at least twelve hours later, when the pains would begin, first annoying, then excruciating. But no one who took it would be alive within twenty-four hours of ingestion."

My mind was racing as I listened to Lindavar's tale. No wonder Benelaius had advised me against drinking the water in Ghars. Blackweed, just like the poison Benelaius had extracted from Mayor Tobald. But who would try to poison Tobald and then . . .

The word suddenly came back to me. *Extracted*, Benelaius had said. But what did he mean, exactly?

"There was enough blackweed in that vial," Lindavar said, "to kill the entire population of a town the size of Ghars, along with whatever important guests were visiting the town at the time."

"The council!" Barthelm cried, leaping to his feet.

"Please, Barthelm," Benelaius said. "All is in hand. Sit and allow Lindavar to complete our case against the killer." Barthelm sat, but he was trembling, and his face looked ashen.

"The Iron Throne wants revenge on Cormyr for its banishment. And what better way," said Lindavar, "for it to drive a stake through this kingdom's heart and strengthen its own trading powers than by assassinating the entire Grand Council of Cormyr's Merchants' Guild? And by something as simple and certain as the ceremonial drink of welcome each member of the council would take upon entering Ghars. The fate of kingdoms depends on more than just the fate of kings. Cormyr's trading position would be thrown into chaos, and the Iron Throne could establish a foothold that might never be broken."

Shortshanks raised a hand. He looked ill and was holding his hand to his stomach. All of the others appeared equally distraught, and even the sun-burnished faces of the Purple Dragons looked pale. "What did you do with the poison?" Shortshanks asked.

"We replaced the vial in the traitor's possession, so that he would not know we had found it."

"Wait a minute!" Rolf said, turning toward old Khlerat and pointing at him. "It had to get into the water supply for it to work, and he's the one who's in charge of the water!"

"Khlerat is not the killer," said Benelaius. It

seemed that he chose to speak only when people needed reassuring. "And don't worry. None of you have been poisoned. Before the vial was returned, it was thoroughly cleansed and the poison was replaced with a harmless crystal."

"A crystal?" asked Rolf. "Wouldn't the killer see that?"

"A crystalline powder," Lindavar clarified, as I considered the possibility that Rolf had little room to be calling other people stupid. "One that dissolved in water as invisibly as the poison. Now," he said, "who drank from the water supply in Ghars this day?"

Everyone except for Benelaius, Lindavar, Kendra, and me raised their hands, all of them uncomfortably. Even the one I now knew was to be identified as the killer did. He probably thought it his last chance.

"Benelaius, Kendra, and myself," said Lindavar, "were not in Ghars today, and Jasper was told not to drink any water there." The young mage went to the first brazier and partially covered it so that only a small amount of light leaked out. He did the same with the others, so that the light remaining was similar to that of a nearly dead fire, enough for us to see each other's forms but no details of face or clothing.

"The crystal we used as a replacement," Lindavar said when we were in near darkness, "was discovered by Benelaius."

"There is nothing of magic in it," my master said, and I heard pride in his voice. "It is a perfectly safe, natural compound derived from crystalline rock. Its main quality is luminescence." He opened his mouth wide, and a ghostly, blue-green circle appeared. "As you see, it shows itself most clearly in the mucous membranes, such as the inside of the mouth and the bowels. If I were to be eviscerated and turned inside-out, I would be quite a sight."

I considered that that would be quite a sight even if he wasn't luminescent, but did not offer the observation.

"So open your mouths, everyone," Lindavar said. "And the outcome will be obvious. The person whose mouth is not glowing did not drink from the Ghars water supply today, even though everyone here, with the noted exceptions, declared that they did so. That person is not only the attempted assassin of the entire Cormyrean Merchant's Guild council and the citizens of Ghars but the successful killer of Dovo and Grodoveth. So open. Open wide, I pray you. . . ."

And they did. One by one, irregular blue-green moons appeared in the darkness of the piazza, except for one person who sat, mouth clamped shut. The Purple Dragons were a row of luminous spheres, and those seated provided a jagged constellation of cool fire.

But on Benelaius's right, there was only darkness, the outline of a figure, a hunched shape that bespoke fear, refusal, and yes, malignancy.

Then Benelaius's voice spoke coldly. "What is the matter, Lord Mayor? Afraid you'll get a mosquito in your mouth?"

32

"Open your mouth, sir, or my men will do it for you," said Captain Flim, his voice as rough and grizzled as his beard.

Mayor Tobald hesitated only another moment, then opened his mouth. It was merely a darker hole in the darkness of his face. I heard the click of his teeth as his mouth slammed shut again.

"Khlerat," said Lindavar, "when I spoke of the poison several minutes ago, you were the first to be alarmed. Is it because you knew that someone other than yourself had access to the cistern today?"

"Y . . . yessir," Khlerat said.

"And who was it?"

"Mayor Tobald, sir. He wished to examine it to make sure all was well for the arrival of the council."

"And let me guess—he told you not to bother, that he could examine it himself without you accompanying him."

"Yessir. That's right, sir. Just like you say." I could

see Khlerat's head nodding just the way that Marmwitz's had, and hoped I didn't come down with such fear-of-authority palsy when I reached their age.

"Did anyone else have access to the cistern today?"

"No, sir."

"Could anyone have gotten to the water supply without your knowing about it?"

"Absolutely not, sir!" That was more like it. There was life in the old boy yet.

"How odd," said Lindavar with more than a touch of sarcasm, "that the only person who had the opportunity to poison the water supply is the only person who did not drink from it today. A dark mouth, Mayor Tobald, is not the thing to have this night."

"Nor is a pronounced limp," said Benelaius, "which I noticed as you entered, Lord Mayor. A limp possibly due to the fact that you have not been taking your gout medicine, which I had prescribed for you and which Jasper had delivered. Could it be that you didn't take your remaining pills because you didn't have them? Because you dropped them on the floor of the cave where Grodoveth was killed, and where Jasper later found them crushed? You said you were never in that cave, Lord Mayor. So how did the pills come to be there?"

The form next to my master had begun trembling, the shoulders hunching as if in the grip of a terrible rage. The Purple Dragons, caught up in the drama, were gripping the hilts of their swords, as was Captain Flim, who had moved nearer the mayor. "Is that everything, sir?" Flim said, his voice cold with anger.

"One thing more," said Benelaius, displacing Grimalkin just long enough to reach into his robe and come out with a small metal oval. He held it up, and in the dim light I could just see the symbol etched into its surface:

"This was found with the vial of poison. It is the sigil of the Iron Throne."

A wordless cry of rage started to bubble up from Tobald's throat as he got to his feet. Unintelligible at first, it transformed itself into words. "You wretch! You meddling old fool! *You* should have been the first to die!"

"I suspect it would have gone more smoothly for you if I had," said Benelaius gently.

"Here stands the killer and the traitor," Lindavar pronounced. "A man willing to murder not only the council but everyone in the town—all the people who trusted him as their leader—in order to aid the Iron Throne."

"The orders from Suzail," Barthelm said, and his deep tones sounded like the voice of doom, "were to have this monster put to death immediately."

"That was the order of the king's court," said Benelaius.

"And it shall be done," Captain Flim said, starting to move toward Tobald, who, in his shivering rage, resembled a blood-bloated spider, ready to run from the fist that is crashing down.

Then a great many things happened. I saw all the cats by the braziers move at once, and the low bowls toppled from their stands, the coals gleaming brightly for a second as they met the air. But their lights were extinguished as they fell over the rail and landed on the ground just below. The piazza and all upon it were instantly thrust into a black, clinging darkness, and I heard the rattle of arms as the Purple Dragons moved to cut off Tobald's escape.

They were too late. The traitor's chair had been

placed by the single opening through the railing to the swamp, and Tobald had instantly bolted when the braziers toppled, taking his chances with the swamp and the darkness rather than his executioners. Try as I might, I could not hear his escaping footfalls over the clatter of the blindly seeking soldiers.

"Stand still!" Captain Flim called. "A light! Someone make a light!" After what seemed like an eternity, I saw a feeble glow inside the door of the cottage, and Lindavar came out bearing a hooded lantern that slowly grew brighter as its oil ignited.

Several Purple Dragons were clustered at the gate, staring into the rapidly fading blackness. Captain Flim pointed a gloved hand and shouted, "There!"

I saw the dim and shadowy figure of Tobald then. He was moving into the Vast Swamp, and, during our search for a light, had gone nearly a hundred yards through the mire. He seemed to be moving slowly, his feet sticking in the black ooze, but he pulled his boots out and continued to stumble on, toward the heart of the swamp.

"After him!" Captain Flim cried, and his men complied, following him down the few stairs that led from the piazza to the ground, but Benelaius called after them, and Flim paused.

"Wait!" Benelaius said. "Not without a light. There are sinkholes and quicksand everywhere." Lindavar passed down the light to Flim, but as I looked out at the swamp, I could see that Tobald was already nearly lost in the darkness.

It didn't stop Captain Flim, though, who moved as quickly as he could through the muck, his men behind him. If he could keep Tobald in sight, I had no doubt that the soldiers would apprehend him.

But then the light of the lantern started to fade, not from any gust of wind, but as though someone were slowly turning off the oil supply. Flim paused to examine it but jerked his head up again when Rolf shouted, "Look!"

Something was beginning to glow out in the Vast Swamp, at the spot where I had last seen the vanishing form of Tobald, and I could see that it was the figure of a man. Even from a hundred yards away, he looked like a giant.

In the cold blue light that radiated from his entire frame, I saw a mane of long hair falling about his shoulders, a gleaming shirt of mail over a broad, muscular torso, and legs as thick as tree trunks. The features of his face seemed magnified by the eerie light that streamed from him. His cheeks were gaunt, his mouth looked as though it had never smiled, and his eyes . . . let me just say that they had seen things I pray mine never have to look upon.

The sight of him was bad enough, and the huge war axe he held effortlessly in his right hand made him not a whit less frightening. "Fastred's ghost," Benelaius said, and although I heard no fear in his voice, I could tell he was as surprised as the rest of us at the appearance of the apparition.

The sight had frozen the Purple Dragons in their tracks, and I could see their forms against the constantly brightening light the ghost exuded. I could also see Tobald.

He was standing only a few feet away from the ghost. My fear at seeing the ghost at a distance was so great that I could only imagine Tobald's terror at such proximity to the creature. He was brightly illuminated by the blue light of the ghost itself, and I saw him throw up his hands as if to ward it off. He stood there, face-to-face with it for a long time. Then it took a step toward him.

Tobald backed away, his head still up, transfixed by the apparition's baleful glare. His arms were up as well, as though he were being accosted by a highwayman. But Fastred's ghost was far more terrible than any mortal brigand.

The ghost advanced, and Tobald continued to back away, until I saw his left foot sink into the black ooze. His fear had usurped his strength. He could not pull his foot out, could only step back with his right foot as well, so that now he was completely mired in the clinging muck.

Slowly he sank down but did not take his eyes away from the unhurriedly pursuing wraith. He never looked down once, but kept his gaze fixed on the ghost of Fastred that now stood directly over him, its axe by its side, watching the man sink lower and lower into the mire.

Soon only Tobald's head and hands were visible, the fingers moving feebly as they were sucked under one at a time. Then there was just his face, and finally that vanished too, like a tiny moon eclipsed fully, sliding ever so slowly into the dark sky.

The ghost looked down at the mire into which Tobald, his lungs filled with swamp mud, had gone forever. Then the phosphorescence that had surrounded the ghost began to fade, while the light of the lantern Captain Flim was holding was reborn and began to grow brighter, as though the light from the ghost were flowing into the living man's lantern. Within seconds, Fastred's ghost had vanished, leaving the vista of the Vast Swamp empty and black once again. We saw nothing but mire and dead trees, and heard only the voices of the night.

At last the silence was broken by the still, soft voice of Benelaius. "I think," he said, "that the orders from Suzail have been carried out."

And none of us could disagree with him.

33

Needless to say, after Tobald sank to the bottom of the Vast Swamp and Fastred's ghost returned to wherever it is ghosts return to after they've finished with their supernatural vengeance, things calmed down quite a bit.

Captain Flim and his Purple Dragons came back onto the piazza, and Lindavar and I brought new coals and relit the braziers so that we had light once again. Once the ghostly chill was gone, everyone was congratulating Lindavar and Benelaius, and even me. Mayella Meadowbrock told me that she thought I had done "a simply wonderful job," but from the way that Rolf was looking at me, I merely thanked her without extending the conversation.

Barthelm was the happiest of the lot, and I thought he was going to fall to his knees and kiss the hem of the two wizards' robes in gratitude for saving the lives of the Grand Council. "Rest assured that I shall see to it that everyone in Cormyr knows of your

genius, young man," he told Lindavar, and I suspected that any negative impressions his fellow War
Wizards might have had of their new colleague
would disappear as quickly as . . . well, as a ghost,
when news of his deductive triumph reached them.
His reputation would be enhanced a hundredfold,
especially since Benelaius kept implying that all the
deductions were Lindavar's.

In truth, I thought it all too possible, especially
when I considered the piece that didn't fit.

I was dying to ask Benelaius about it. After everyone but Lindavar and Kendra had left for Ghars, I
approached him in his study. "Master," I said, "there
is still one thing that I would like to ask you about."

He held up a hand and shook his head. "Our guests
leave tomorrow morning," he said, "and it is quite
late. There will be plenty of time on the morrow to tie
up . . . loose ends, Jasper. Now, get you to bed for a
well-deserved rest."

The finality of his last sentence allowed for no
objection, and I wearily went upstairs. Yet despite my
tiredness, it took a long time for me to fall asleep. The
terror of the ghost was still fresh in my mind, but
what really kept me awake was my certainty that
Lindavar's deductions were not totally correct. Oh,
yes, Tobald was the traitor all right. His placing what
he thought was poison in the public cistern was proof
of that, along with his outburst at Benelaius once he
had been found out.

But what haunted me more than any ghost was the
thought of the pills that I had delivered to Tobald that
very morning.

*   *   *   *   *

The next day dawned without its usual dryness and

sunlight. Dark clouds had gathered on the horizon over the swamp, and a brisk wind sent them scudding northwest, toward us and, hopefully, the farms beyond.

I was the first awake in the cottage, and when I went downstairs I saw Kendra sleeping on the chaise, beneath a coverlet of cats. She looked quite comfortable, and I heard her snoring softly.

In the kitchen, I pushed the window open and let the strong wind blow in. It brought a fine mist of water with it. Good. It had begun to drizzle. With luck, rain would follow. I breathed in the damp air, trying to get myself awake and alert for the day. Both Lindavar and Kendra were leaving, and I wanted to send them off with a good breakfast. Then, once they were on the road, I could at last talk to Benelaius.

By the time the others were up and dressed, I had a sumptuous repast ready for them, and they feasted triumphantly. I, on the other hand, only picked at my food, my mind far away from the needs of my stomach.

"Jasper," Benelaius said heartily, "here you've made us this fine breakfast and you hardly touch it yourself. Come, come. Eat up, or the cats will have the better share."

"Very well, master." I made myself smile and nod, and managed to get down a few bites of griddle cakes and sausage, but I could not get my questions out of my mind.

Lindavar was the first to leave at midmorning, by which time a gentle rain was falling. Benelaius and his former pupil bade each other an affectionate farewell, Lindavar climbed into the carriage, and we were off, with my master and Kendra waving goodbye.

As I turned my head and saw Benelaius and

Kendra standing there, looking perfectly natural together under the umbrella he was holding, I realized that I didn't know if Benelaius had ever been married, or had a woman in his life. There was much I did not know about him, and a few things that I must either learn about or go mad.

Lindavar and I spoke seldom on our journey. What little he did say had to do with thanking me for all my legwork. "Were it not for you, Jasper," he said, "I fear that Ghars might be a town of the dead today."

That was excessive praise, and I told him so, but I did not mention what was bothering me. That was for Benelaius's ears only.

The rain kept everyone in Ghars indoors, except for the few who were overjoyed at the sheer novelty of it. The council was deep in its meeting, and I saw none of the honored, and nearly murdered, visitors. I wondered if Barthelm would apprise them of how closely their lives had hung in the balance, but then decided that he would not. Telling your guests that they had narrowly missed suffering a slow and painful death is not the best way to impress them with the hospitality of your town.

I waited with Lindavar in the soft rain until the coach for Suzail arrived, and we said a friendly goodbye. "Look after Benelaius, Jasper," he said, taking my hand. "He's a great man, good and wise, but he needs someone like you. And thank you for your hospitality as well as his. It was . . . an interesting stay."

He grinned, climbed into the coach, and gave me a wave as it rolled away toward Suzail and the College of War Wizards.

I drove the carriage back to the cottage as quickly as the horses could go, and when I put Jenkus and Stubbins in the stable, I noticed that Kendra's horse was gone. Inside, I found Benelaius alone, seated before the fireplace on the chaise in which Kendra had slept, and absentmindedly stroking the cats that had settled on his lap. He scarcely seemed to notice me when I came in.

"Has the lady left, then?" I asked him.

"Left?" His voice was faraway, and when he looked up at me, so were his eyes. "Oh, yes, she has." He touched his cheek, as if remembering something soft and foreign that had rested there. "She had to ride on. Heading for Anauroch, I believe. Something about a lost city filled with jewels." He gave a bittersweet smile. "I've had a full life, Jasper, but sometimes I realize that there are things that I have missed."

He inhaled sharply, as if clearing his head. When he looked at me again, his gaze was now on me and nowhere else, and he smiled and spoke crisply. "Did you get Lindavar off to Suzail?"

"Yes, the coach left promptly. He's on his way back."

"Good, good, and with a much greater reputation than he had previously. This little affair should make some of the more hidebound wizards in the college look at him as more of an equal. And what's more, he did it with his wits. Not a bit of magic."

"And did you do it with your wits, too, master?"

He cocked his head as if I'd just made a jest he didn't understand. "I beg your pardon."

"Something's wrong and you know it," I said. "You knew last night when I mentioned a piece of the puzzle that didn't fit. What about the—"

"The pills," he said, smiling benignly, "of course." My mouth fell open for an instant, and I shut it again. "I knew that you were certain to realize that piece didn't fit. I trusted, however, that you would remain silent and let us play it out, and you did."

"Tobald was out of pills the morning Grodoveth was murdered," I said, trying to put it into words. "But he had his pills yesterday morning. I took them to him myself. So why was he limping last night?"

"Because of Razor," he said, tickling the temperamental cat under the chin so that it purred in delight. "Razor bit him as he entered, you see. Hard. Right on the ankle. Enough to make anyone limp. I knew Tobald wouldn't say anything about the bite, because of what you had told me about his attempt to impress Mayella Meadowbrock with his supposed camaraderie with animals. He would have lost face with her were he to let anyone know that he alone of all who traipsed through my house was the only one unlikable enough to be bitten." He shook his head. "Odd, isn't it? As far as he knew, he had already poisoned her, and yet he couldn't bear to have her think him a man so base that animals hated him. Ah, vanity."

"You planned for Razor to bite him?"

"Jasper, my communication with my pets is, shall we say, intense. We need no words, my dears and I."

"But why did you want Tobald to limp?"

"So that everyone would think he dropped his gout pills in the cave and stepped on them."

"But I hadn't delivered the pills to him yet. He didn't have them to lose in the cave."

"Of course not, Jasper. But *I* did."

"What!"

"Yes, I followed Grodoveth to the cave, you see— I'm not completely sedentary, no matter what you might think—and there I found him dead. No one else was in the cave. Except Fastred, of course."

My head was swimming. "What are you . . . mean . . . Tobald didn't kill Grodoveth?"

Benelaius shook his head.

"Then, for the gods' sake, who did?"

"The same person who killed Dovo." I tried to keep track of the conversation, but it seemed to be skittering all over the place like a salamander in a skillet. I'm afraid my confusion showed on my face.

"Evidence can be manipulated in certain ways, Jasper," Benelaius said patiently. "It's almost like magic, but not real magic. It's more like prestidigitation, using misdirection to show you only what I want to show you and nothing else. You think a ball or a scarf has vanished into thin air, but it hasn't. It only looks that way. Your Camber Fosrick—or any good detective—can make a situation look exactly like he wants it to."

This so-called explanation wasn't helping a bit, and I told him so. "Are you saying," I asked him, "that you framed an innocent man?"

"Bite your tongue," he answered in mock dismay. "I framed no one who was not already a traitor and an attempted murderer . . . mass murderer, for want of a better term." Benelaius's face grew grim. "Tobald's poison would have slain hundreds of people. The vultures would have feasted in the streets of Ghars for weeks to come. Men, women, even children and babes in arms, all would have died in agony. No, Tobald deserved far worse than the fate that he met in the swamp."

His face brightened a bit then, and he looked up at me and smiled. "And speaking of the swamp, I think the best way for you to understand what truly happened is to go there with me. You shall be the student, and I the teacher, just as we are during your tutoring sessions. I shall ask you questions, and you shall ask me questions, and thusly, by asking and answering, you shall derive your knowledge, yes?"

"If that's the only way to get to the bottom of all this, yes, of course."

"Excellent. Then briskly make us a light lunch to fortify us against the rigors of the swamp, and your questions will be answered and your puzzles solved."

34

I felt as though it was the slowest lunch ever made by the hands of man. The fire took forever to bring the water to a boil, the meats took an eternity to fry, the soup eons to bubble. But at last the meal was served, and slowly and appreciatively eaten by my master. For myself, I could scarcely get down a mouthful, so huge was the lump of expectation in my throat.

After he finished eating, Benelaius pushed himself back from the table, stifled a small belch, and stood. "You seem somewhat anxious to have your questions answered, Jasper. Therefore, why not clean up the dishes when we return? I am sure the cats will do an excellent job of erasing most of the remaining bits and sauces so that your later cleanup should be minimal."

I couldn't have thought of a better idea myself. He told me to get two lanterns, and then, to my surprise, told me to saddle Jenkus and Stubbins rather than hitch them to the carriage. "Are you sure, sir?" I said.

"Do you think me incapable of riding a horse?" Benelaius said, somewhat piqued. "I was, after all, a War Wizard, lest you forget, and Stubbins is a gentle creature, when one knows how to approach him."

He wasn't gentle when I saddled him. He twisted and kicked in his stall so that I was afraid he would break several of my bones before I could cinch him. But Benelaius showed up, clad in an oilskin rain cloak with a hood, and spoke softly to Stubbins so that I was able to finish my work and lead him outside.

Benelaius didn't hesitate. He swung himself into the saddle, and Stubbins stood beneath him as placidly as a windless pond. "Well?" Benelaius said. "Are you too stunned by the sight of a real equestrian to get mounted yourself?"

We headed west on the swamp road in the drizzling rain. For all his girth, Benelaius sat his horse well. I began asking questions immediately.

"How on earth did you ever wind up at Fastred's tomb?" was the first one.

"Through following the lead of Grodoveth. As you know, he was our primary suspect from the beginning. First of all, he was left-handed—"

"Which Tobald wasn't," I said.

"That's correct. But since Tobald was unschooled in the arts of war, he might very well have swung an axe forehand rather than backhand. But that's neither here nor there. It's Grodoveth we're concerned with now. He had the means and the opportunity but not a motive, as far as I could see. And frankly, I wasn't quite sure that I wanted to find it, if it existed."

"Why not?"

"Answer the question for yourself, pupil."

225

I thought for a moment. "Possibly his position? I mean, he was a relative of the king himself."

"Precisely. By marriage, true, but still on the fringe of the royal family. To convict him, or even to question him, would have taken overwhelming evidence. And even then it would put the royal family in such a bad light that it might not be worth the effort.

"You may recall a case well over a hundred years ago in Waterdeep, Jasper, in which a relative of the queen was suspected of killing several wenches in a thoroughly unpleasant manner. But the fact that he was even suspect came out only in recent years. Fortunately, before he came into line for succession to the throne, he died in battle. Fleeing, I believe. So it all worked out nicely."

"Are you saying it would be better to let a murderer go free rather than cast aspersions on the crown?"

"That is a moral dilemma I am glad we did not have to face. Now, last night I stated that Grodoveth had an interest in the history of Ghars, and possibly Fastred in particular. But because, as you found out, he had been investigating those legends *before* the bogus ghost started to appear, what assumption was it logical to make?"

"That he had something to do with the ghost."

"Of course. Now there *are* such things as coincidences, but when one is looking for connections, one takes what one can get. So it seemed likely at the time that Grodoveth was in some way responsible for the hauntings. He had the brains and the wheretofore that Dovo did not. The most likely result of the hauntings, and one that anyone might expect, would be to keep people away from the swamp. Therefore, the next question is?"

"Why would Grodoveth want people kept away from the swamp?"

Benelaius nodded, and rain dripped from his hood onto his lap. He brushed away the water patiently. "As the broken lantern and its disappearance would suggest, Dovo was signaling to someone on the other side of the swamp. And what is there?"

"Sembia." I wondered if I was going to get a grade on all this.

"And when one thinks of illegal doings in Sembia, one naturally thinks of the Iron Throne. So there at least was a premise from which to start. Dovo was sending messages to Iron Throne agents. But what kind of messages? 'Wish you were here? Bring rain?' Hardly likely."

"And the ghost appeared," I said, "when Grodoveth was staying in Ghars."

"That's right. And the trade information that he possessed would be invaluable to the Iron Throne."

I tried to work it out with words, but it was difficult. "So Grodoveth told Tobald, and Tobald told Dovo, and Dovo told the Iron Throne agents with lantern signals. But that's pretty much what you said last night."

"Yes, but you've just added a middle man. Tobald."

"But . . . but he was in on it, wasn't he? I mean, you proved that last night."

"Yes, he was. But you see, Tobald didn't have to tell Dovo. Can you see why?"

Then I had it. "Because Grodoveth told Dovo." I pulled back on Jenkus's reins and stared at Benelaius, who also reined in. "You mean . . . they were in it together?"

"Of course they were," my master said. "Can we continue, please? This is a day for answers, not for standing still and chatting in the rain." And we rode on.

35

"There was a bond between the two," Benelaius said, "far deeper than that of master and student. They were both familiar with disgrace. You already know about Grodoveth's displeasing the king with his lechery in Suzail, but did it never occur to you that Tobald's leaving the university when he did was mildly suspicious?

"Most university masters remain there for their whole lives, writing when they tire of teaching. But Tobald left in what one would imagine to be the prime of his academic life, at an age when others would not only be highly acclaimed professors but would also have established themselves as scholars in their fields, beginning to create bodies of literary work. Yet Tobald left Suzail and came to little Ghars, where he immediately became a large fish in a tiny pond.

"We may never know what exactly it was that caused the university to dismiss him. It might have been something as simple as sloth. But it really doesn't matter. What matters is his response, which was the same as Grodoveth's. They felt no disgrace, only dishonor. In their own eyes, they had not done wrong; the wrongs had been done to them by those more powerful than they. In Tobald's case, the university, and in Grodoveth's, King Azoun himself. And so?" Benelaius said, suggesting that I continue.

"And so they brooded," I said, trying to imagine what went on in these two men's minds. "They grew angry, and eventually they wanted revenge."

"Mmm. Revenge on the universities, on their king, on their country itself. Enough of a motive for the overthrow of Cormyr, by military . . . or economic means."

"So when someone from the Iron Throne approached Grodoveth," I ventured, "he was ripe for the picking. He had probably found a sympathetic ear in Tobald from the start, and shared the plot with him." I looked sharply at Benelaius. "What do you think the Iron Throne promised them in exchange for their betrayal of their country?"

My master shrugged. "Riches, undoubtedly. The Iron Throne and Sembia would realize great wealth as a result of Cormyr's economic woes. Perhaps Grodoveth and Tobald even looked forward to the possibility of an eventual Sembian invasion of Cormyr, depending on how much damage was done to the kingdom. Then—a puppet throne for Grodoveth, and Tobald's revenge on those in the university system who he felt had wronged him. We'll never know what they had in mind, but we can be grateful it did not come to fruition."

By now, we were passing the Swamp Rat, and Benelaius nodded toward it. "Feel a need to take the damp out of your bones?"

"Not in there," I said, thinking of the weak ale and the pickled eggs. Then I happened to remember something. "But Grodoveth did, though, didn't he?"

"Did he?" the wizard asked slyly.

"Of course. When he spent the night there, he knew exactly what room to go to without asking, because he had done so before. The Swamp Rat was their base of operations, wasn't it?"

Benelaius only smiled, and returned my question with another. "If it was, do you think Hesketh Pratt, the good proprietor, was apprised of the plot?"

"No. It nearly ruined his business. An axe-swinging ghost is hardly a drawing card." We traveled another hundred yards as I thought through the scenario. "Grodoveth or Tobald would give Dovo the information, either in town or at the Swamp Rat, and then Dovo would ride out to where the path led into the swamp, hide his horse, scare away any passersby who might have seen him, and then go off with his lantern into the swamp." I looked at Benelaius, suddenly puzzled. "But why then did I find his cloak and hat at the Bold Bard?"

"Why do you think? Would he have left them there?"

"No," I replied after a moment's thought. "But Grodoveth or Tobald might have."

"And why?"

"To throw suspicion on Shortshanks perhaps, or at any rate to draw it away from the Swamp Rat. But why the whole plot in the first place, master? Why couldn't Grodoveth just pass the information on himself?"

"A king's envoy is an important person, and important people are under far greater scrutiny all the time than are mere blacksmith's assistants. Grodoveth could disappear long enough to speak to Dovo, or perhaps the lad came to Tobald's house after dark and received his information there. But it was necessary to have a third party. Too, if Dovo was caught, he could easily have said he was playing ghost for fun. Whatever Grodoveth and Tobald were paying him would have been worth the mild punishment he would receive. Now come."

Benelaius turned Stubbins off the road and down the hill toward the spot where I had found Dovo's corpse. "We are here. We'll tie the horses and then walk in to the tomb."

"Can you . . . I mean, do you think you should, master?"

He answered petulantly. "I did before, didn't I? In the darkness of early dawn and followed by a traitor. I suppose I can do so now in broad daylight followed by"—his tone abruptly softened—"a friend and helper."

"How did you find this place?" I asked as we started back into the swamp.

"The same way Grodoveth did. In his studies into the legend of Fastred, undertaken at first in order to provide a cover for his messenger, he learned more and more of the tales of Fastred's tomb, and the treasure that was supposed to be there. By comparing dozens of cross-references, and by a few leaps of intellect, he was able to pinpoint not only the location of the tomb, but also how to open it.

"When I learned from you what books he had consulted, I simply did the same reading in my own library and came to the same conclusion. I solved the riddle early in the morning of the day Grodoveth was found dead, and rode Stubbins out here, tying him where he wouldn't be seen."

I remembered hearing the cottage door close that morning. "That *was* you then, returning about seven thirty. And out here is where Stubbins got the mud on him."

Benelaius nodded. "I'm afraid I'm not very adept at rubbing down horses. At any rate, as soon as it was barely light enough to see where my feet would land, I started in on the path that was visible to one who knew where to look.

"But very shortly I began to hear footfalls behind me. At first I thought it was a creature of the swamp, and that I might have to resort to a protective spell, which would have been an admission of defeat after going all these months without using magic. Fortunately, I didn't have to. But I'd better tell you why a bit later. As you can see, there is a thornslinger just ahead."

I didn't need to be reminded. I remembered the terrible violence of the tree all too well. We passed it in near silence, the only sound the soft sucking of our boots on the muddy surface of the path. When we were a good distance away, Benelaius resumed his tale.

"When I heard someone following me, I walked faster, naturally. In fact, I was running, not a frequent occurrence, I may tell you. Before long, I came upon the mere . . . ah, there it is just ahead of us. At least a half mile across, wouldn't you say? I have a theory that we should test when we have more time. Across that mere is another path, else the Iron Throne agent never should have gotten there. I suspect it leads through the swamp to the southeast, all the way to Sembia. But we shan't journey to that country today."

He turned left on the path that ringed the mere, and I followed him toward Fastred's tomb.

"The path led directly to the mound," he said, "and I hid behind it, hoping against hope that my pursuer just happened to be going to the same place as I.

Miraculously, such was the case. It was Grodoveth, as I saw from the brush where I was concealed. I had no choice but to lie down, and I'm afraid I got my cloak rather muddy."

"So that was it," I said, remembering the last laundry I had washed. "It didn't get muddy from just rubbing against Lindavar's clothes."

"No, and my apologies for making you work so hard at your washing. Grodoveth grinned when he saw the mound, and at first I was afraid he was grinning at me, prior to playing bobbing for wizards in the quicksand. But he didn't even know I was there. He fumbled about on top of the mound for a moment. I heard the click of a long-hidden latch and saw him opening a trapdoor buried by thick layers of moss and swamp slime. Then he descended the stairs into the tomb. Ah, and speak of the wicked, here it is."

The mound was there, sodden with the rain. The trapdoor on top was still open, just as we had left it, and I wondered if any creatures had descended to try and make a feast on Fastred's dry corpse within. Remembering the bare bones, I knew they would find slim pickings, unless they had remained to await the advent of a corpulent wizard and his servant.

"There is where I hid," said Benelaius, pointing to a large, low, needle-leafed bush. "In a moment, I heard noises. There was a sharp, singing sound, then a clatter of something, but no voices, not even a groan. After waiting a bit longer and hearing only silence, I decided to investigate. At the bottom of the stairs I found Grodoveth in the same bisected condition in which you saw him later that morning, the axe precisely where you found it." He gestured downward. "Come, let us revisit the scene."

"Are you sure it's safe?" I asked him.

"No one would go down there without a light," Benelaius said, "and it seems quite dark."

"I wasn't necessarily thinking about humans," I said.

Benelaius only laughed and lit one of the lanterns, while I lit the other. Then he began to walk down the slippery, moss-covered steps. I followed.

36

At the bottom were two dried areas of blood, the larger one where Grodoveth's body had fallen, and the smaller one where his head and shoulder had lain. A passageway led into the dark room where Fastred's bones sat upright.

"There lay the body, there lay the axe, and there"—he pointed at the passageway—"was darkness. I entered that room, and found only the body of Fastred, with a small box at his feet. There was no one else. No possible killer."

"Not Tobald."

"No. But what I saw, and what you might have seen, told me that the same person had killed both Dovo and Grodoveth. Look, Jasper, and observe."

Frustrated beyond words, I did as he asked, and covered the floor even more carefully than I had before. "Cold . . ." he muttered. "Colder . . . a bit warmer . . . warmer . . ."

"Master, there is nothing on the floor!" I blurted out.

"Then look up, Jasper. Behold what is right before your eyes."

I examined the wall, and my attention was once again captured by what I had taken to be a line of striation in the rock. Since it was the only thing I saw on the wall, I touched it and discovered that what I had thought a thin layer of rock was actually damp clay. "Very hot now," said Benelaius as I dug the clay away from the rock.

When I had finished, I had discovered a concealed trap. It was horizontal, an inch high, two feet deep, and five feet long. When I held my lantern to one end, I could make out a heavy metal spring that pointed toward me.

"There's more to it than it appears," said Benelaius. "A rather clever contraption for being five hundred years old. And it did what it was set to do. It killed the first intruder to enter Fastred's tomb."

"But . . . but I thought you said the same person who killed Dovo killed Grodoveth."

"And so he did. After all, it was Grodoveth whose foot snapped the cord that sprung the trap that beheaded him, much the same way that he beheaded Dovo after he and Tobald heard the man bragging in the Bold Bard. The motive was what I stated last night, though the perpetrator was the one with the military training. Tobald would have made a botch of beheading.

"And Grodoveth's own beheading was less than clean. The axe came out of the wall before he had time to react and, well, you saw the results."

"Yes," I said, "and I saw other things, too, things that I didn't recognize at the time. The axe was chipped where it hit the stone floor after passing through Grodoveth's body, and the two gouges on the handle were from where it had lain in its holder all those centuries, the pressure of the spring cutting into the wood. And when the spring was released, it cut into the handle even more deeply, exposing the wood underneath." I shook my head, angry at myself. "I wondered at the time why Fastred's axe wasn't buried with him. I should have realized that it was, that it guarded his tomb. I should have seen it."

"Don't be too hard on yourself. You entered with presuppositions in mind. I was fortunate enough to enter seeing precisely what happened. I must confess that my curiosity got the better of me then, and I searched Grodoveth's garments. In them I found a vial of poison identical to the one I later found in Tobald's cloak while I was examining him. It seems the Iron Throne was taking no chances. Oh, I didn't need to analyze it, since blackweed has a very distinctive odor when found in such a concentrated dose. And when I found the Iron Throne sigil as well, it all fell together."

"Grodoveth had a sigil, too?"

"Not *too*. Tobald didn't have one, at least not on him. As you recall, I stated only that the sigil was found with the vial of poison, and that was true."

I suddenly remembered another fancy bit of wordplay. "The same way you said you 'extracted' the poison, not from Tobald's blood but from his cloak. And when we learned that it was poison, and you said that you 'gave him something for it,' you meant you replaced it with the crystal."

"Precisely. Well done, Jasper. Camber Fosrick would be proud of you."

"But why didn't Tobald have a sigil if he was working with the Iron Throne?" I asked.

"Oh, I suspect he did, but Tobald was never as

bold as Grodoveth, who logically never expected to be searched. I imagine the Purple Dragons will find a similar sigil among Tobald's possessions in his home, carefully hidden away somewhere."

I looked at our footprints on the floor, and the opening in the wall from which the axe had come flying out. "Then the footprints that I saw here of the heavy man were yours. But I don't understand why you hid the trap with clay."

"Because once I found incriminating evidence on Grodoveth's body," Benelaius said, "I immediately suspected that Tobald might be in league with him. They were, after all, inseparable when Grodoveth visited Ghars, and my assumption did prove correct. I suppose the plot to make it look like Tobald was solely responsible was forming itself in my brain even then."

"Then that was why you left the pills on the floor."

"The pills?" He looked up absentmindedly. "Oh, yes, even I lose things from time to time."

"Crushing them was a nice touch," I said with a smirk.

"Indeed. Too obvious otherwise. It was necessary, you see, that Tobald was believed to be the killer and no one else. After all, Grodoveth had already paid for his crimes with his life, and it would be a great disgrace to the throne were the king's cousin-by-marriage to be proven a traitor. But this way he can be remembered as a loyal servant of the king. It was necessary that Tobald, who was equally as great a traitor, and had every intention of destroying his own town in order to kill the merchants, pay for Grodoveth's crimes as well."

"But why was Tobald so anxious to have the killer found, particularly since the orders were instant death?"

"That was especially why he wanted him found. Tobald didn't know how Grodoveth was killed. He probably thought that someone had learned about their plot, followed Grodoveth to Fastred's tomb, and killed him. Speaking of which, the tomb must have come as quite a surprise to Tobald, since I doubt that Grodoveth shared that particular information with him. He sought the tomb for the reputed treasure, and I'm certain his partnership with Tobald would not have extended to sharing the gems."

"So for all Tobald knew," I said, "whoever killed Grodoveth might be targeting him next."

Benelaius nodded. "And the faster that person was executed, the less he would be able to reveal about Tobald and Grodoveth's connection with the Iron Throne, assuming he knew about it. No, Vangerdahast's order played right into Tobald's hands, or so he thought."

"Because," I went on, "the last thing he expected was to be accused himself, especially with the wealth of evidence that you provided." I gave a dry laugh. "He must have been doubly furious at you, for he knew that you had manufactured much of it."

"But I did not manufacture his intent, nor his treachery. I feel no guilt for what I did, Jasper. Justice triumphed. 'Bought with blood, paid for with blood.' That is the legend in this tomb, and it provides an apt epitaph for Grodoveth and Tobald."

I eyed Benelaius thoughtfully. "You talk a good talk, master, but you're not as bloodthirsty as you let on. You wanted Tobald to escape."

That produced an elevation of his bushy eyebrows. "And what makes you say that?"

"That eight cats would accidentally overturn four

braziers at once strains the limits of credulity. You had them do it on purpose, signaling them in some way. That was why you had Tobald sit by the opening off the piazza."

Benelaius's face grew wistful. "I dislike bloodshed, Jasper. I would have particularly disliked the sight of a man—any man—hanging from a tree near my cottage. Yes, I would have preferred Tobald to escape, for to whom would he have fled? The Iron Throne? Even if he could have gotten through the swamp, he would have been of no further use to them. On the contrary, he would have been a failure, and they might have killed him because of it. In truth, I expected him to flee into the swamp, where he would eventually be pulled down by the mire. That it happened the way it did was, I must confess, a surprise to me."

The memory of Fastred's ghost made me think once again of the tomb in which we stood, and I realized that there was still one more unanswered question. "The treasure," I said. "You took it, didn't you?"

Benelaius waved a dismissive hand and smiled beatifically. "Put the treasure from your mind as I have from mine. You need know only that Dovo's long-suffering family will suffer no longer. They will shortly receive an extremely generous inheritance from a distant relative of whose existence they were not even aware. And to add to their happy ending, two traitors have been punished, a plot against Cormyr scuttled, and the haunting of the swamp at an end . . . at least from Fastred."

Just as we turned to walk back up the stairs, we heard a sound from within the inner tomb. It was a dry rattle, like a fortune-teller casting the bones onto a tabletop over and over again.

Or like an ancient skeleton, walking for the first time, and swiftly.

37

"I think someone's awake," Benelaius said softly, but I could hear the concern in his voice.

I was more than concerned. My eyes felt as though they were the size of saucers, and my sudden freshets of sweat had just doubled the normal humidity of the swamp. But I couldn't move until Benelaius grabbed my arm and started up the stairs. "I suggest we leave," he said, and I didn't have to be told twice.

By the time we had grappled our way up the slick and mossy steps, abandoning our lanterns in our rush, I heard the clattering bones at the bottom. In spite of myself, I turned and looked down.

It was the skeleton of Fastred all right, clad in armor, helm, and rotting boots. The gray day illuminated him poorly, but twin fires burned in the hollow eye sockets. The glare held me captive, and I could only watch as he began to ascend the stairs, the leather strips of boot dropping aside as the bony toes dug into the moss. I knew that I would stand there until he was at the top of the stairs, taking my thin neck between his finger bones and squeezing and squeezing until my eyes *were* as big as saucers, saucers popping right out of my head. . . .

And then I felt a clout on the side of that selfsame head that jerked my gaze away, breaking the bonds that held me to the dead thing. "Run!" shouted Benelaius. "Now!"

I did as my master ordered. I ran, knowing from his past teachings that what followed us was not truly Fastred's ghost. *That* we had seen the night before, while this was only some wandering evil spirit that had entered his bones in order to wreak havoc among the living. Still, that knowledge was cold comfort as we squished our way along the trail, having to watch every step and yet move as quickly as we could. A single misstep would bring disaster, for the sound of rattling bones drew ever nearer.

"Master," I panted, "wouldn't it be . . . a good idea . . . to work . . . a spell?"

He moved fast for a stout man, and I was amazed that he was able to speak without panting. "As you know, I would prefer to avoid using magic, Jasper."

"We may not . . . have that choice . . . master," I replied, feeling a hot burning creeping up my sides as I ran.

"Just a bit farther," he said, beginning to sound winded himself. "Make sure you do . . . whatever I do."

I grunted in affirmation and pressed on, not daring to look over my shoulder. I had no idea where we were, or how far we had to go to get to solid land, or even if that would do us any good.

What I did know was that we had no chance of outdistancing the evil thing behind us. The clattering was growing louder and closer, and suddenly I felt something sharp like the point of a spear rake across my back, tearing my cloak and my shirt and the flesh beneath.

The pain spurred me on, but I knew I couldn't last much longer. Skeletal fingers plucked again at my back, and I nearly fell, when Benelaius suddenly shrieked at the top of his lungs. When I looked, I saw that he was diving belly-first onto the swampy ground.

Make sure you do whatever I do.

And I dove, too, just sliding under the barrage of thorns that whizzed through the air toward us.

Benelaius had shouted to alarm the thornslinger, and that deadly tree had launched dozens of its lethal missiles in our direction. We struck the earth just in time, but the living horror that inhabited Fastred's bones was not so lucky.

I rolled when I hit the mud, and saw the thorns take the monster. They pierced the ancient armor, splintered the brittle bones, and shattered the yellow, moldering skull into four pieces that flew in separate directions as the split helm rolled to a stop by my feet.

In seconds, what had been a running nightmare became a pile of harmless rubble, spread out over a wide area. Most of the bones sank quickly into the mire, but a large chunk of rib cage landed over a dead log, where it moved for a long time, the ribs twitching like separate fingers.

At last I looked slowly at Benelaius, who smiled, put a finger to his lips, and said, so softly that I could barely hear, "Shhh . . ."

We got to our feet, and I picked up the helm.

Then we walked slowly and carefully out of the thornslinger's range toward the road and safety. When we were a hundred yards away from the final resting place of Fastred's bones, Benelaius turned back toward me. "All right, then," he said with a great sigh, "*now* Fastred's haunting of the swamp is at an end."

"Better late than never," I said with a smile. "What was that thing, anyway? A wandering spirit?"

"I imagine so. A good lesson for us. Always leave tomb doors closed. You never know what might come in and possess your corpse." I made a mental note of it. Then Benelaius glanced at the ruined helm in my hand. "A souvenir?"

"Yes, I thought."

"That's fine . . . as long as whatever might be left of Fastred doesn't want it back."

I thought for a moment, then tossed the helm on a muddy rise and didn't look back at it as we trekked on toward dry ground.

Jenkus and Stubbins were never a more welcome sight, and we mounted and headed back to the cottage. The rain was falling more heavily now. "It seems that the drought will shortly be over," Benelaius said.

"If this continues."

My master looked up at the sky, sniffed the air, then nodded. "It will." I didn't ask him how he knew, but I wanted to learn. He had not yet taught me the secrets of the weather.

"You know, it's a shame," I said, "that no one will ever know the truth. You really should record the events for posterity."

"I leave that to you, Jasper. Your vocabulary is certainly up to the task, and your recording skills are as fine as most scribes. Write it down if you will, but it must be a tale that cannot be told for many years."

"Does Lindavar know the entire truth?"

"Unfortunately, no. I had to keep it secret from both of you so that your . . . performances would be believable. Besides, Lindavar's success will not only improve the way his fellow War Wizards look upon him, but will also bolster his image of himself."

"It's too bad that he takes all the credit when you really solved the mystery," I said, and chuckled. "Instead of the 'consulting cogitator,' you could become famed as the 'cogitating conjurer!' "

"Please . . ." Benelaius moaned, then added lightly, "I no longer need such recognition. Besides, the nature of men being what it is, I am sure that there will be many more crimes to investigate in the future, even in a sleepy little town such as Ghars."

By the time we arrived home, the rain was falling heavily. I stabled the horses, then went inside to find Benelaius unaccustomedly piling up logs in a haphazard manner in the fireplace as the cats watched curiously. "Thought a nice fire would banish the dampness," he said, putting a large log on top so that the pyramid toppled over, scattering the cats in every direction.

I laughed and said, "Well, if you'll just wait until I get our muddy clothes soaking in some water, I'll build a fire, master."

He straightened up and gave me one of his serious looks. "First of all, you don't have to wash the clothes; secondly, you don't have to build the fire—I should be learning how to do these things for myself; and thirdly, you need not call me 'master.' "

Then I remembered what, in the exciting rush of the last several days, I had forgotten. "My indentured service to you," I said. "It's over today."

"It is," said Benelaius briskly. "And although I shall be sorry to see you go, I know that you have been looking forward to your economic and social freedom. You may feel free to spend the night here, of course, or longer, and leave whenever it suits you."

I didn't know what to say. The joy I had expected to feel on this day had been replaced by another kind of joy, that of having helped to accomplish a great task, of having been the legs and eyes and ears of a great man, one who had taught me much, who had made me into a different person, and who could teach me still more.

Lindavar had asked me to look after Benelaius, had said that he needed someone like me. And I thought that maybe I needed him as well.

For a while longer, at least. It had proven to be quite an exciting week, and for all I knew there could be more excitement to come. If not, at least I would continue with a splendid education from one of the greatest men of the age. All in all, not a bad deal.

"Master . . . uh, Benelaius . . . did you say you were sorry to see me go?"

"I did. You are bright, alert, and you cook far better than I. I particularly relish your sausages. . . ."

"Would you be willing then to let me remain in your employ without an indenture? As a salaried employee?"

Benelaius tried to look slightly surprised, but I saw that he was feigning. "I do pay you a salary, Jasper. A silver falcon a month."

"And if you wish me to remain . . . Benelaius, you shall pay me twenty silver falcons a month."

The startled expression on his face was sincere. "Oh, now I hardly think that—"

"Farewell, then."

"What about five?"

"What about twenty?"

"Oh, come, Jasper, we can surely bargain . . ."

"Fine. Let's start bargaining at twenty."

"Seven?"

"You like doing your own laundry?"

"Nine?"

"Feeding all the cats?"

"Twelve?"

"Caring for the horses?"

"Fifteen?"

"Mucking out the stables?"

"Eighteen?"

"Emptying your own chamber pot?"

"All right, then, twenty!"

But I had only begun. "Cooking? Washing the dishes? Going into Ghars for supplies?"

"Twenty-five, then! And not a copper more!"

"A deal!" I cried, and grasped his hand and shook it.

He shook his head ruefully. "I see that halfling blood in you all too clearly," he said. "Very well, then, wash up our cloaks, then build me a fire, make me some tea . . . and bring in the books on invertebrate species. We've neglected your studies for far too long."

I grinned and made him a slight bow. Soon there would be a fire in the fireplace and a pot of tea on the hob. I swept up the muddy cloaks under one arm and proceeded to the washtub in the kitchen, whistling cheerily and petting hordes of purring cats as I went.

I was home.

R.A. Salvatore

The *New York Times* best-selling author of the Dark Elf saga returns to the FORGOTTEN REALMS® with an all new novel of high adventure and intrigue!

the
SILENT
BLADE

Wulfgar's world is crumbling around him while the assassin Entreri and the drow mercenary Jarlaxle are gaining power in Calimport. But Entreri isn't interested in power—all he wants is a final showdown with the dark elf known as Drizzt. . . . An all new hardcover, available October 1998.

FANTASY ADVENTURE

Ed Greenwood's
The Temptation of
Elminster

The third book in the epic history of the greatest mage in the history of Faerûn.

The glory that was Cormanthyr is no more. The mighty city of Myth Drannor lies in ruin, and the still young Elminster finds himself an apprentice to a new, human mistress. A mistress with her own plans for her young student. Tempted by power, magic, and arcane knowledge, Elminster fights wizard duels, and a battle with his own conscience. Available in hardcover, December 1998!

Island of Elves

Elaine Cunningham

The millennia-old history of the center of elven culture. What draw does this tranquil island have on Faerûn's elves? What does the future hold for this ancient and elegant race? From the long-forgotten struggles of the elven gods to the abandonment of the forest kingdoms of Faerûn, *Evermeet* is a sweeping tale of history, destiny, and fate. Available now in hardcover.

The Netheril Trilogy
Sword Play
Dangerous Games
Mortal Consequences
Clayton Emery

The barbarian Sunbright's destiny becomes entwined with the decadent archwizards of the Empire of Netheril and the course of the history of Faerûn is changed forever! *Available Now!*

The climax of the FORGOTTEN REALMS's longest running series . . .

The Harpers 16
Thornhold
Elaine Cunningham

An order of paladins is about to fall at the hands of the Zhentarim, and the young Harper agent sent by Khelben to stop it comes face-to-face with her own destiny. A birthright that may mean the end of the Harpers! *Available August 1998.*

. . . and the beginning of the next great series . . .

Lost Empires
The Lost Library of Cormanthyr
Mel Odom

Baylee is a finder of lost treasures. When his mentor and friend is murdered, it's up to Baylee to finish the old man's greatest quest . . . to find a secret repository of the arcane knowledge of the ancient elven empire. But Baylee isn't the only one looking for it, and something very powerful will do anything to protect it.

Faces of Deception
Troy Denning

Atreus, a young nobleman driven from his home, is hidden with a disfiguring spell that has kept him alive, but made his face a twisted mockery of human. Only in the faraway realms of the Utter East can Atreus find the secret to reversing the spell. *Available November 1998.*

FANTASY ADVENTURE

CRUCIBLE:
THE TRIAL of CYRIC the MAD
Troy Denning

The time has come for the gods of Toril to bring the mad god into line for the good of the world and all its people. But on this world, the gods are far from infallible. . . . The eagerly awaited sequel to *Prince of Lies*, by the *New York Times* best-selling author of *Waterdeep*. The legacy of the Avatar continues!

Edited by Philip Athans

An anthology of all new FORGOTTEN REALMS stories by **Ed Greenwood, Elaine Cunningham, Jeff Grubb, James Lowder, Mary H. Herbert, J. Robert King**, and a host of other talented authors that bring you tales of murder, intrigue, and suspense in the strange world of Faerûn. A world where detectives can Speak with Dead, and villains can animate a victim's corpse and have it cover the clues to its own murder. A world where the mystery story takes on a whole new dimension. . . .

the
Shadow
Stone
Richard Baker

A young apprentice wizard is confronted by the corrupting influence of power gone mad. Now, against all odds, he must stop his teachers from ripping the world apart with their unquenchable thirst for evil. The first in a new series of stand-alone novels: FORGOTTEN REALMS Adventures!

Available September 1998